Why Johnny Died

Why Johnny Died

Marlis Day

Pittsburgh, PA.

ISBN 1-56315-184-7

Paperback Fiction
© Copyright 1999 Marlis Day
All rights reserved
First Printing - 1999
Second Printing - 2000
Library of Congress #98-85301

Request for information should be addressed to:

SterlingHouse Publisher, Inc.
The Sterling Building
440 Friday Road
Pittsburgh, PA 15209
www.sterlinghousepublisher.com

Cover design: Stephen Czarnecki and Michelle Vennare- SterlingHouse Publisher
Typesetting: Michelle Vennare - SterlingHouse Publisher

This is a work of fiction. Names, characters, places, and incidents either are the
product of the author's imagination or are used fictitiously. Any resemblance to actual
events or persons, living or dead is entirely coincidental.

Printed in Canada

This book is dedicated to the memory of my mother, who shared her great love of literature with me, to my husband D.J. and my children, Stephanie and Joe, Travis and Theresa for their love and support, and to my friend Middy for all her encouragement.

Acknowledgements:

I would like to thank the staff of the Pike County Public Library for their assistance in research, my colleagues, Mike Krieg and Barbara Jochim for help in word processing, my brother and the best English teacher of my acquaintance, John Black, for proof-reading, my brother-in-law Brent Stuckey and friend Russell Mahoney for legal advice, and the many friends who read and made suggestions.

Preface

And what of teaching? Ah, there you have the worst paid and the best rewarded of all the vocations. Dare not to enter it unless you love it. For the vast majority of men and women it has no promise of wealth or fame, but they to whom it is dear for its own sake are among the nobility of mankind. I sing the praise of the Unknown Teacher...

Famous educators plan new systems of pedagogy, but it is the Unknown Teacher who delivers and guides the young. He lives in obscurity and contends with hardship. For him no trumpets blare, no chariots wait, no golden decorations are decreed. He keeps the watch along the borders of darkness and leads the attack on the trenches of ignorance and folly. Patient in his duty, he quickens the indolent, encourages the eager, and steadies the unstable. He communicates his own joy in learning and shares with boys and girls the best treasures of his mind. He lights many candles which in later years will shine back to cheer him. This is his reward.

Knowledge may be gained from books; but the love of knowledge is transmitted only by personal contact. No one has deserved better of the Republic than the Unknown Teacher. No one is more worthy to be enrolled in a democratic aristocracy—king of himself and servant of Mankind.

—HENRY VAN DYKE

We are not always happy when we smile.

—James Whitcomb Riley—

Chapter One

Seventh graders didn't die . . . it was the first time in my twenty years of teaching that one of my students had died. There had been a few summer accidents through-out the years involving children from our school, but death had never visited my classroom until that day.

When the announcement reached the school that morning, the faculty was visibly shaken. The seventh graders were called into the auditorium at the beginning of first period and were given the despairing news by a solemn Dr. Fitzbaum, the school principal.

James Whitcomb Riley Middle-High School housed nearly twelve hundred pupils and engaged the talents of some eighty teachers, not to mention the secretarial, cooking, and cleaning staff. Three principals stood at the helm of our great vessel. Dr. Leo Fitzbaum, our main building principal, hired, fired, and evaluated us. He attended hearings concerning truant or wayward students and presided over faculty meetings and graduations.

A middle-aged man with a jaded countenance, Leo was neither feared nor loved by his underlings. Balding and slightly paunchy, he bordered perilously on nerdness and looked forever in need of a pair of suspenders to hold up his baggy pants. In whispered tones, the students referred to Dr. Fitzbaum as "Old Fuzz Ball." They thought we didn't know; but we always knew. Since he was almost totally charm-free, I figured he was the grand wazoo simply because he had the most stripes on his sleeve.

Dr. Fitzbaum looked old and stern as he addressed the assemblage of students. Apparently, seventh-grader Johnny Benson had been bitten by a poisonous snake and had died at home during the night. A terrible accident and tragedy. A floral arrangement had already been sent from the entire school, but if individual classes wanted to order flowers it would be a nice gesture. Students gasped and were respectfully quiet. A few girls wept openly, but most of the youngsters paled and sat in stunned silence.

Pauline Forbes, the plump and tightly-corsetted school counselor, tapped her way to the microphone on tiny four-inch spike heels, defying gravity with every step. She attempted a feeble bit of group counseling and reminded the students in a tremulous voice that her door was always open, if anyone wanted to come in and talk about it.

The formidable Mr. Claude Dupree then strutted with an almost military demeanor to the podium and discussed the dangers of snake handling and reptiles in general. An assistant principal, Mr. Dupree was mostly in charge of discipline. Ever on patrol, he roamed the halls relentlessly and frequented all athletic events in his quest of perpetrators. His tactics were legendary, and no ground was sacred to Mr. Dupree. In his pursuits, he had even been known to thrust his nose into the girls' restroom whiffing for smoke.

A Viet-Nam veteran, the compelling Claude was prompt, neat, and highly efficient in all his duties. When a perpetrator was apprehended, Mr. Dupree would strike like an avenging thunderbolt; justice was unfailingly swift and severe. His forte was his tall, lean, muscular body, and clothes were probably his only vice.

Each day he appeared early and was dressed in coordinated outfits like a model out of a Lands End catalog. He was the only man I ever knew who actually tied his sweater sleeves around his shoulders. He projected himself as a superior member of the species, but his well-trimmed dark mustache gave him sort of a Nazi look. Most of the faculty saluted Claude Dupree and gave him a wide berth.

Although usually in control, Mr. Dupree was perpetually unnerved by loud, unexpected noises (probably the result of the Nam experience) and was known to leap and bolt at the signaling of fire drills. Once when a playful student tossed a firecracker at a football game, Claude hit the ground spread-eagle and suffered a bloody nose for his efforts. He later claimed that someone pushed him, but those who witnessed it said most profoundly, "Nay, not so, he was expecting a direct hit."

Of course, Mr. Dupree mentioned his Viet Nam experience and the horrific snake bites he had seen. His voice rang with portent. He then flipped out large, colorful charts of dangerous snakes native to our area. All students were emphatically warned, and they trembled in unison.

Our third member of the administrative personnel and the token woman was Frances Updike. A thick-bodied, plain woman, she consistently wore dark skirts with matching blazers as her school uniform. With wire-rimmed glasses, a severe haircut, and no make-up or frills, this austere woman appeared completely sexless. We never were sure of her age, but the kids ascertained that she must have come over on the Mayflower.

The officious Frances had survived an abusive childhood, delinquent children, and a crazy husband—who was rumored to have tried to kill her. Clearly, years of stress and turmoil had made Frances as solid as a rock. The only telltale remnant of her hellacious years was a cruel tic that manifested itself in a grimace that occurred periodically.

When least expected and usually without provocation,

Frances would wrinkle her nose, clamp her teeth together tightly, and pull back her lips as far as possible. During that time, her eyes always took on a glazed and slightly wild look. It usually lasted only two or three long seconds. Adults who had known Frances for the long haul ignored it, but it always scared children and strangers. When it passed, she would resume her composure and dialogue as if nothing had happened.

Nothing earthly could shake her; she thrived on crisis. She would listen for hours to anyone who claimed a problem and dole out sympathy in mega-doses. Her province was curriculum, but her specialty was dysfunction.

Besides counseling and carrying around large stacks of paper, we never were quite sure what Frances did. Angry parents were usually routed over to Frances, and hours later they stumbled out of the building bleary-eyed and worn down. But old Frances was always there for us. Never too busy. No problem was ever too small to consume an entire day.

When Mrs. Updike failed to follow her colleagues to the microphone and exhort on the dangers of the natural world, I assumed she had been left to hold down the fort in the office area. However, another teacher informed me that good old Frances, (with tic in full force), was already en route to the Benson home, hell-bent on delivering comfort and with enough food trays to feed a third world. We could only imagine how the already grieved family would react to her unseemly affliction.

For most of the kids, it was the first time that death had taken a peer. Only old people died. They felt vulnerable and betrayed. We had a moment of silence for Johnny and then filed silently back to class.

Death was always a shock, but a child's death seemed so pointless and unfair. Where were the parents? Where was God? Were the angels still singing?

In class, it seemed therapeutic to let the students talk about Johnny. Some recalled the last time they had seen him; others remembered the last words they had spoken to him. Everybody appeared to have fond memories to share: a discussion at lunch, sharing a bus seat, being partners on a field trip, etc. The students decided to each bring a donation the next day for flowers. I readily agreed to call the local florist and have a bouquet sent to the funeral home.

Actually, I knew very little about my deceased student and felt somewhat guilty that I had not taken the time to become better acquainted with him. I remembered a chubby twelve-year old with a big smile. He had always talked so loudly that I had mentioned it to the school nurse and suggested a hearing check. She hastily informed me that his hearing was intact; it was just a long-running habit being worked on by the speech therapist.

After death, we tend to lend perfection to its victims. Actually, most of the kids had had little to do with Johnny. Sadly, he was something of a misfit. His clothes always seemed to be too small and his hair too long. He talked too loudly, and his actions were very immature for his age group. Keeping mostly to himself, he appeared to be in closer touch with the animal world than the real one.

When my students wrote essays, Johnny invariably chose lizards as his topic. When I took my class to the library, he unfailingly selected books about lizards. The students were required to write daily in a journal, and his writings usually included excerpts which confirmed his preoccupation with small reptiles. He had several for pets and drew detailed pictures of them on his notebook. His favorite one was a brown, six-inch skink that he called Ralph. Usually, a tiny sketch of a lizard had accompanied his signature. I did recall noticing the near-obsession with his little reptiles, but let it go thinking it was most likely a passing phase. Twelve-year old boys are often fascinated with the bizarre.

I recalled the third week of school, when Johnny had come to my desk and intiated a conversation about finding Ralph in a funny place the night before. I replied off-handedly, "I'd love to see Ralph sometime."

At that, he quickly reached inside his faded sweatshirt and said in his booming voice, "WELL, HERE HE IS!" As he said those words, he simultaneously displayed before my eyes a six-inch, brown lizard. I nearly fell out of my chair, but strived for composure; teachers develop great skill at theatrics.

"Oh," I replied, "Did you bring him for science class?"

"NO . . . HE JUST LIKES TO COME TO SCHOOL WITH ME!"

"You've brought him before?"

"OH YEAH, HE'S BEEN HERE EVERY DAY THIS YEAR."

"You keep him under your shirt?"

"HE LIKES TO RIDE ON MY SHOULDER, BE-TWEEN MY UNDERSHIRT AND SHIRT."

"Doesn't he need to eat or something?"

"SURE, I BRING FOOD PELLETS AND WATER." At this, he whipped out a small, plastic sandwich bag and dumped onto my desk small, brown pellets and the tiniest water bottle I had ever seen. (The label said BEANO.)

"When do you feed him?"

"EVERY MORNING DURING YOUR THIRD PE-RIOD CLASS AND IN MR. BARRINGER'S SIXTH PERIOD SOCIAL STUDIES CLASS."

I gasped, and I'm sure my eyebrows hit my hairline for

the second time in those few unexpected minutes. Lizard-feeding in my class every day! Good grief! What else had been happening in my class without my knowledge? Nonchalantly, I asked, "What do you do with him in gym class?" I knew students were required to change into gym clothes.

"I JUST PUT HIM IN MY BOOK!" At this, he showed me a book which appeared to be normal a first glance. But when he opened it, I could see that a large, oval cavity had been cut very carefully into the thick pile of pages. How ingenious of Johnny, I thought.

"Do any of the other teachers know that you bring him to school every day?" I asked.

"JUST MRS. RAYBURN, MY SCIENCE TEACHER." Roxie. Why had my colleague never shared that with me?

Suddenly, I remembered my class and glanced up. My students sat wide-eyed in astonishment—mouths gaping. I had been so filled with my own near-hysteria that I had forgotten they were even there.

"Did any of you know that Johnny brought Ralph to school every day?" I asked with forced calmness. One shy girl's hand went up hesitantly. She blushed . . . another socially challenged child. I did not pursue the questioning . . . to her great relief.

"Hey, can we bring pets to school?" a loud-mouthed boy inquired boisterously.

"I believe you have an assignment to do; please get busy," I replied authoritatively. Rank does have its privileges.

When lunch period arrived that day, I hurried off to find Roxie Rayburn, science teacher and lizard co-conspirator. "Did you know that Johnny Benson brought a LIZARD to school every day under his shirt?" I asked quizzically, as I unwrapped my tuna sandwich.

"As a matter of fact, I did," she retorted calmly. "He

doesn't bother anyone or even show anyone. It's sort of like a security blanket to him." She sipped on a diet Coke.

"Did it not occur to you to have him ask a principal if it was okay?" I asked professionally.

"Naw, they'd have just told him no, and they let much worse stuff go on around here every day," she replied so convincingly that I agreed. "They'd have called him down to the office, and it would have scared him to death. I feel rather sorry for the little guy; he seems so lonely." We spoke no more of it.

Friendships among teachers were usually based on logistics more than politics. When two teachers were thrown together at prep time AND lunch, fierce, loyal friendships evolved. Such it was with Roxie and me. We found each other the first week of school and hit it off immediately. Being a science teacher, she was from another pod; but she compensated. Since both of us were avid readers, we had much in common from the genesis of our alliance.

She and her husband, Denzil, an old hippie artist who worked out of their home, had lived in the county for twenty-plus years and knew nearly everyone. His specialty was environmental art, and his wood carvings of ducks were displayed every year at the county arts festival. The only child of their union was a red-haired daughter named Liberty. A free-spirited marine biologist, she had been called to the sunny beaches of Florida.

Roxie wore environmental T-shirts to school, more to bug the NRA proponents than for the actual cause. They were a group who frequented the teachers' lounge and boasted about their hunting prowess. Deer, rabbits, squirrels, quail, and doves fell to their deadly arrows. Being an animal lover, Roxie found their hobby despicable. They claimed it to be great sport, while she maintained that it would be more of a sport if the little creatures had weapons too.

It was always a trip to see Roxie each morning. She unfailingly wore costumes rather than clothes and planned her accessories in great detail. Her usual get-up consisted of an oversized environmental T-shirt and matching leggings or stirrup pants. Ankle chains decked both ankles, and she wore three earrings in each lobe. As a nod to convention, the top holes always got gold and the middle ones bore her birthstone; but the bottom ones were grandly versatile. These were usually seasonal: ghosts, turkeys, Christmas trees, bunnies, or flags—depending on the current holiday. My personal favorites were the exact replicas of eyeballs that she always wore on "Be Kind to Your Eyes" week.

Her short, curly hair is chestnut-brown and her oversized glasses cover most of her face. Going to college in the sixties had taken its toll on Roxie, and I always suspected that she had a tattoo. Most likely, a dragon or a smoking gun was carefully concealed under her stirrup pants.

With her husky voice and slight drawl, she'd occasionally spin into phases that were definitely foreign to us. Once she referred to her lunch sack as her "poke," and when we all looked at her questioningly, she retorted, "Well, hells-bells . . . I'm from West Virginia."

My name is Margo Brown, and I teach language arts to seventh graders in the only middle-high school in Riley County. Our school draws students from three small towns and all the rural areas in between. I'm not a native, and when I first began traveling over the river from a neighboring county to do my good work like a missionary, I was very suspect. It was as though I had just arrived from the North Star. But after twelve years of proving my good intentions, I was munificiently accepted into the private and secret world of the gentle folk who dwelt there.

I never planned to be a detective—it was just in the

cards dealt to me that fall by Providence. My husband, Dewey Douglas Brown, better known as "Dew-Drop," teaches biology in an adjoining county. Ours is a good life, challenging, but dotted with vacation days.

Our children, Leigh and Will, had escaped to freedom during the past two years and were actively engaged in college life. Visits home were sporadic and becoming fewer and farther between. Although we missed them, Dew and I were enjoying our new-found freedom and were basking in the peace on the homefront.

We live in a rustic country home that we built fifteen years ago in the middle of our wooded acreage. Our phone rarely rings; our laundry has been reduced drastically; groceries last forever; and we can both actually park our vehicles in the garage. Age does bring its own rewards.

That evening as Dew was barbecuing thick hamburgers for our supper, he tried to console me. "You have over one hundred students in and out of your classroom daily, Margo. There's no way you can get personally involved with each of them. You have no reason to feel guilty."

As I sliced some of our last garden tomatoes onto paper plates, I lamented, "But if I had shown more interest in his lizards, maybe we would have gotten around to discussing snakes." I settled onto a picnic bench and propped my feet on the deck railing.

"Let it go, Margo, you can't be responsible for what happens to your students when they're at home. We can't be their parents and teach them everything they should know. We'd probably be stunned if we knew what happens in the lives of some of our students."

He piled some soft margarine into his steaming baked potato as he spoke. I knew he was right; I would make a call at the funeral home and try to put it all behind me.

But I still didn't feel absolved of my guilt . . . my sins of omission.

James Whitcomb Riley Middle-High School was built during the passing phase of the "open concept." As most educational trends, it passed away into oblivion almost as suddenly as it was born; and we were left with a large, open school built on the premise of an expensive pole-barn.

A normal day at JWR vaguely resembled a large family reunion or a small revolution in progress. Some students would be roaming about, others sitting in large groups attempting to write or read, while others were conducting scientific experiments or watching films on literature or history. Needless to say, youngsters who were supposed to be watching the war films were usually watching the compelling science demonstrations; and those who were in science class were inevitably engrossed in the hoopla of a nearby spelling bee. Focusing became a problem of monumental proportions.

When it became obvious that no one was learning anything, the community cried, "Foul!" and back we went to the old, trusted system of classrooms. As the anxious teachers garnered corners to call their own, they created make-shift walls of bookcases and portable chalkboards. Sound was still a problem, and voices became louder and louder as was necessary to overcome the din of war films and music classes. Eventually partial walls were built, but large open doorways still encouraged the noise factor.

The school was structured around the "pod" idea, and nine square sections were joined by ramps and walkways. Each section became almost like a small old-fashioned school with its own group of teachers. In the middle of each section, a meeting place was established where teachers could plan, grade papers, and store information.

Of course, teachers, being natural nesters, purchased

small refrigerators and microwave ovens for their areas. They stored soft drinks, coffee, crackers, cookies, micro- wave lunches and popcorn. Presto! Instant lunchrooms were born.

There was great bonding among the teachers in each pod, and gossip was inevitably carried from pod to pod by visiting nurses and substitute teachers. The school be- came a collection of islands in the sea of education.

There were three thirty-minute lunch periods, and a teacher could draw a different eating time each year. A grand, almost familial camaraderie developed between lunch groupies. In addition to lunch, every teacher had a "prep" period daily or a period with no class assignment. It was magnanimously designed for grading papers and preparing lesson plans.

The teachers' lounge was a popular place each period as the group of "free" teachers came in to exchange edu- cational ideas and share philosophical revelations. Some brought stacks of papers to grade. For others, it was merely a time of rest and relaxation.

Several pieces of rump-sprung vinyl furniture formed seating groups in the center of the lounge. Soft-drink and candy machines lined one wall, while a triple-pot, chrome Bunn coffee maker graced another. Quarters were tossed into a small wicker basket on the honor sys- tem. Some had little honor; others made change diligently. Our mailboxes were also in the lounge, so it was mandatory to check in at least once a day.

By some tacit agreement, the teachers' lounge was just that, and administrators rarely darkened the door. As the academic year wound down, attitudes therein digressed from Lords of Academia to Peking Man. To observe the teachers' lounge and its diverse occupants was a true study of human nature.

With the unraveling of the school year, the room di- minished from neat to disorderly. Under stress, weary teachers wadded papers and shot at wastebaskets during the second semester. Misses were rarely picked up by throwees. Sarcasm came easily in March as duress mounted. By April, pop cans were being bounced off walls, and many cheers and hi-fives were heard when a difficult shot was made. Lunch debris became unspeakable as surly teachers ate like refugees. Two hundred pound teachers with glazed eyes were seen walking on the furniture in May rather than detouring around it, or asking a colleague to move. Summer vacation always arrived just in time to save the lounge from total demolition by professionals.

Most of the faculty members were amiable. There were the former jocks, who coached passionately and took little else seriously. They wore baseball caps and taught in jogging suits and leather Nike shoes. One peculiar trademark of the coaching staff was their jaunty gait. Without exception, they walked on their toes, as if they had sore heels caused from sprinting down too many athletic fields.

A group of ulta-professionals were constantly attending seminars in an effort to improve their teaching, while rewriting curriculum to upgrade the entire demeanor of the system. Naturally, they were eager to share their newest revelations with the entire faculty. They spoke with rapture at regularly scheduled in-service meetings and appeared remarkably undaunted by the frequent yawning and nodding of their disinterested colleagues.

Of course, like every school we had the "burn-outs," those dispirited teachers who had taught too long, but weren't quite old enough, sick enough, or crazy enough to retire. They gravitated towards each other like planets to the sun and did an inordinate amount of grumbling.

But all in all, it was a good group of teachers, and they served as positive role models to many kids in desperate need of one. Most really were concerned about the students and spent their days fervently trying to impress educational concepts into the minds of their wards. Undeniably, the teachers supported and cared for their students and each other, being quick to respond to any crisis in the life of a student or colleague.

Looking back, our students at James Whitcomb Riley Middle-High School had seemed, in some obscure way, to sense the ease with which autumn had glided in and had reflected it in their moods. The school year had gotten off to an easy start. Classes were smaller than usual and kids were relaxed and ready to learn, faces turned up like baby birds. I even recall how nicely the walls bore my welcome-back decorations, and how easily we had all slipped into a contented routine.

For students and teachers alike, each beginning school year is a renaissance, a great new awakening of spirits to achieve more than in previous years. School buildings are shiny-clean from being freshly scrubbed and painted. It is a time of new jeans and Reeboks, fresh haircuts, and crisp new bookbags amply loaded with school supplies. For a few brief weeks each year, education is king.

And so it was that fall, straw-golden days drifting by like leaves in a stream. Students and teachers had become acquainted and education was in full swing, when we received the shocking and tragic news: Johnny Benson had died.

Chapter Two

Roxie hates to drive, so I picked her up the next evening, and we drove to the funeral home in Pleasantville to make a call. In contrast to previous hot and humid Septembers, the days were crisp and promised to be riotously beautiful. As the last days of the month drew near, treetops were already boasting brilliant reds and glinting golds. Skies were azure-blue and flocks of noisy geese were gathering and raucously announcing southern trips. Autumn days were serene and glorious that year . . . for a while.

Although Roxie wore her usual attire, her lowest set of earrings caught my attention. Two-inch, silver dinosaurs swung boldly on metal loops. I was aghast when I realized that each had flashing red eyes. "Johnny loved my tyrannasaurus-rexes," she said calmly. "I wore them for him."

In contrast to Roxie, my appearance is more conventional, and I usually wear skirts or dresses to school at least twice a week. I tell Dew that I just want everyone to remember that I'm a lady. Once blond, my short-cropped hair is light brown with gold highlights. My mother always said that my eyes and hair have become exactly the same color. Since I wear glasses only for reading, I often keep them dangling from a cord around my neck. At five-four, I'm a couple of inches taller than Roxie, but

according to the height/weight charts, we're both a little
too short for our poundage. With birthdates being only
a month apart, we attribute the discrepancy to the slow-
ing metabolism of our age group and wage continual
warfare.

On the way Roxie shared a little personal history on the
Benson family. Johnny's mother had never been married,
and Johnny was her only child. No one knew who the
father was, but it was whispered that she had been "mess-
ing around" with some construction workers who were
passing through the area repairing power stations. Peggy
Benson and her son had lived alone in a trailer at the
edge of town for a while. However, Johnny's widowed
Grandmother Benson didn't think her daughter was a fit
mother, so she had insisted on raising Johnny.

Peggy became angry when the welfare people insisted on
Grandmother's custody and moved away briefly. Unable
to support herself on minimum wages, she had returned
home and lived with her mother and Johnny in a very
modest home near the state forest. During the past year,
the grandmother had died of a heart attack, and Johnny
and his mother had been living ever since that time together and alone. Apparently, with social security and the
grandmother's small nest egg, they had been able to survive. Peggy had been deemed mentally disabled several
years before and also qualified for benefits.

Upon our arrival at Stokeley's Funeral Parlor, I braced
myself. There's nothing worse than viewing the body of
a child, and I dreaded it immensely. All I could think of
was how devastated I would be if it had been Leigh or
Will.

Surprisingly, there were not many people in the spacious, flower-scented room. A few somber people were
milling around examining floral arrangements, and possibly a dozen visitors were seated in the metal folding chairs.
Roxie pointed out Peggy Benson to me, and we solemnly

approached her to express our regrets.

Peggy was probably fifty to sixty pounds overweight; her reddish-brown hair hung limply over her rounded shoulders. She wore no make-up and an ill-fitting, gray polyester suit with a paisley scarf tied about the neck. Her only jewelry was a pair of gold-tone earrings, probably clip-ons. I would have guessed her age to be in the mid-thirties. Her face looked swollen, and her eyes were red-rimmed. My heart went out to her, and I was overwhelmed by a sense of pity. I wished there was a way I could have eased her pain.

We shook her hand and told her how sorry we were about Johnny. She smiled when we told her what a nice boy he had been, and how we had enjoyed having him in our classes. Softly she murmured, "Thank you for coming."

She led us to the casket to pay our respects to Johnny. He looked peaceful and so young and healthy. His hands were folded over his pale blue suit and were holding a small, white Bible. That booming voice silenced forever, I thought, as unshed tears stung the backs of my eyes. I wondered about his lizard, Ralph, but didn't ask.

Looking around, we saw the flowers sent by the school and the various classes. An arrangement of fall flowers with several neighbors' names had been placed near the casket, along with one from a local church; there weren't many more. Two planters sat on a piano, and one had a small angel attached to it.

We sat near the door and spoke to several teachers who came through repeating our pattern. It seemed barbaric to display the family so publicly in such a time of grief; but it is our cultural heritage, this ancient ritual of displaying the dead.

Evidently, Johnny didn't have much family. Of course, since the father and all of his relatives were non-existent that made a marked difference. One young couple up front reportedly were cousins of Peggy, and a pair of older ladies were maiden aunts, sisters to Peggy's mother. This family could have held their reunions in a mini-van.

It surprised me to see our school secretary, Franny Bumpus, weeping copiously near the casket. Thinking she must have just been extremely tender-hearted, I mentioned it to Roxie. She then informed me that Franny was Peggy's older sister, but they had been estranged for years. Another fact no one had ever bothered to tell me, I thought.

Belatedly, I realized she had been absent from school on both Thursday and Friday, but I hadn't connected it. Franny was divorced and was probably around forty. She had been the main secretary to the principals at JWR for almost twenty years and was most proficient at her duties.

Franny, even at forty, still had a voluptuous body. Her large, unwieldy breasts were enhanced by the tiny waist, which she kept cinched in at all times. I often wondered if she slept in a tight, wide belt. As she walked, she swung her rounded hips almost to a beat. Her long, painted nails and assortment of flashy rings didn't seem to interfere with her typing prowess. Although she appeared to be the perfect stereotype of the dumb-blond . . . she was truly efficient.

In addition to typing and filing for the administrative personnel, Franny called substitutes for the absentee teachers and kept accurate track of everyone. Undeniably, she did her job well and possessed an uncanny ability to calculate when a crisis would surface. She was first to know about births, deaths, and other crises and responded appropriately in behalf of the school. Her expertise merited her a special parking slot near the front doors of the building. Franny didn't forget; telling Franny was like carving it in stone. However, I often mused that her blond, frizzy hair appeared as though she had cleaned her toaster without remembering to disconnect it.

Educators measure time in academic years rather than calendar years; the main topic among the group of teachers near us was in regard to relegating the proper classes to the Benson girls. It was finally settled upon that Franny had been a member of the senior class of 1974-75, and Peggy had been with the 1980-81 scholars. Bingo! My age-guess was right on target.

According to their memories, Franny had been an excellent student, showing great promise for higher education, but Peggy had suffered from a learning disability. Although she had been in regular classes, she had received special help from the LD teachers from early on. In whispered tones, they agreed that she was MMR (Mildly Mentally Retarded).

And now, I thought, she had lost the only thing she probably had ever had or would ever have. The flowers and soft music did little to dispel the melancholy we all felt. We sat in quiet reverence for probably thirty minutes, and then we began our leave-taking by twos and threes.

As Roxie and I stepped out onto the porch of the Victorian funeral parlor, the crisp evening air was tainted by cigarette smoke. The smoker was standing with his back to us and had a cowboy boot propped up on the porch railing. As he heard the door close, he turned and faced us. It was the deputy sheriff, Sonny Ray Haggard. He was a tall, scruffy man, friendly but with a lot of bravado.

Everyone knew the local law enforcement officials in small communities. Their jobs included supervising the school crossings, apprehending traffic offenders and vandalizers, discussing drug abuse at P.T.A. meetings, getting cats out of trees, providing security for all school athletic events, leading in parades, and directing traffic flow at community activities.

Sonny Ray was somewhere between thirty-five and forty years old and had been a deputy sheriff ever since his father, Burley, had become the county sheriff. Riley

Countians truly liked Burley R. Haggard; he was a "good old boy," and always ready to assist them. They tolerated the turkey-brained Sonny Ray simply out of respect for his father. The Haggards had been the main local law enforcement officials ever since I began working in Riley County and probably long before then.

Sonny Ray had a prominent forehead which made him appear rather cerebral, but it was just an illusion. He wore rather thick glasses; I ascertained that he had probably burned his retinas out staring at the sun. People said that his poor eyesight had given him a somewhat skewed version of reality. Fancying himself as a ladies' man, he was twice divorced and usually had several current lovers.

Supposedly, he and his first wife had two small children when she left him and went back to her hometown in Arkansas. Apparently, she had forfeited child support when she remarried under the condition that she and her children never lay eyes on him again. However, Burley and Mrs. Haggard faithfully made a yearly pilgrimage to Arkansas with gifts and good grandparently intentions.

"Evening, ladies," drawled the willowy Sonny Ray.

Roxie spoke first. "How ya' doin', Sonny Ray?"

"Me, I'm doin' fine, myself, but I shore do feel for Peggy right about now. Ya' know, when she called me to come, I just had this bad omen that it was something real bad. And shore enough, when I got there, there was that little ole' boy dead, with his arm all swole' up, and that rattlesnake still in the room."

"How did it get in there?" Roxie asked in a puzzled tone.

"Well, I reckon he just brought it in there, thinking it was harmless. Ya' know he was always out in the forest huntin' up lizards and stuff like that. He always brought them into his room and played with them."

"Had no one ever talked to him about poisonous

snakes?" I inquired. Johnny was a bright boy; I couldn't imagine him being so naive.

"I reckon they had, but you know how boys are—they don't listen very good. Hell, I was like that myself—had to take my lumps the hard way." We had no trouble believing that.

He then took long draws on his cigarette, and we watched as he allowed the smoke to flow out of his mouth only to be inhaled up into his nostrils, like twin smoky rivers. He undoubtedly thought we'd find it sexy. Instead, I felt suddenly nauseous.

"See ya', Sonny Ray," said Roxie.

"Take care, ladies," replied Sonny Ray. "And don't do nothing I wouldn't do . . . Ha!" I silently figured that must about cover everything.

Driving home, Roxie and I were silent, shrouded with an exhausting, draining feeling that made us both feel old and sad and thankful that it was Friday. We hoped that maybe by Monday we'd get ourselves and our classes back to normal . . . life does go on. We knew a service was to be held for Johnny on Saturday, but we did not feel obliged to attend. It seemed a kindness to let the family and few neighbors and friends have their final moments with Johnny in privacy.

Sleep did not come easily that night; dreams were dismal and inflated with caskets and images of lizards. But when I awoke, I somehow knew what I needed to do to fill the huge void within me.

As with all my other students, Johnny's journal sat on the shelf in my classroom. He had written his thoughts down, as per my request, every day since school had started. It was a common practice for students to keep journals in language arts classes, and to write in them daily. Sometimes the students wrote about the events of the day or the previous day; often they wrote poetry or anecdotes. At other times, they chose a topic from a list of "story starters" which was stapled onto the cover of the journal. Typical topics included: My Favorite Holiday, Five Things That I Love, What Makes Me Angry, If I Had Three Wishes, etc. Teachers didn't grade the writing or criticize it. It was merely a way to encourage students to write.

As the school year progressed, kids usually became most adept at expressing their thoughts on paper. Teachers generally checked over the journals diligently every two weeks or so and wrote encouraging comments. After the first week of school, I had scanned over the writings and offered cheerful remarks. All I recalled about Johnny's was that he had an inordinate amount of knowledge regarding lizards.

For three weeks, I had not read any journals; we had been so busy getting the academic year rolling. Under ordinary circumstances, I probably would have taken them home with me on Friday and perused them over the weekend.

What else had Johnny written about? His deepest thoughts and last written words would no doubt be a source of comfort to his bereaved family. As I lay under a quilt on that crispy, autumn Saturday morning, I felt absolved by my plan. I would read through Johnny's journal on Monday and learn more about him. A few days later, I would then deliver it personally to his mother. She would always treasure it.

I had such noble intentions. Little did I know what information was waiting for me in the journal and what dire consequences my finding it would cause.

Chapter Three

Monday mornings are always blah. I'm not sure if it's due to too little sleep or too much food over the weekend, but I always wake up on Monday mornings feeling as if I'd sucked on a piece of chalk all night. Hoping to jump-start ourselves, Dew and I sipped hot, high-octane coffee and routinely watched the mundane morning news and weather.

Since neither of us have much appetite in the morning, we breakfasted as usual on TOTAL and orange juice. Not that we were particularly fond of TOTAL, we mused, but because we had neither the capacity nor the time for sixteen bowls of another type of cereal. Actually, since we had officially declared ourselves middle-aged, we had taken an abrupt interest in the preservation of our bodies, had set serious goals for longevity, and had embraced a healthy life-style.

October had gloriously been borne in on a swelling tide of tree-top fire, and the weekend had been crisp and gorgeous. We had taken a ten-mile bike ride on Saturday and visited with friends and neighbors along the way. Twelve-speed bikes made pedaling up the hills tolerable, and our new, spandex biking shorts with the foam-padded seats prevented posterior discomfort. We decided that bicycle seats had gotten much harder as the years had passed.

When I arrived at school, the daily bulletin informed me that a tree was to be planted on the school lawn in memory of our deceased student, Johnny Benson. All seventh grade teachers were instructed to take their students to the east lawn immediately after attendance was taken. My students were thrilled—any opportunity to miss a little class time enthralled them.

As to be expected, Mrs. Updike was in charge of the tree-planting ceremony. Roxie and I shamefully counted tics as Frances stood by the pile of fresh dirt waiting patiently for the bevy of students to respectively assemble. It was a thoughtful gesture and had undoubtedly been solely Frances' idea.

After her fervent and uplifting speech, each child was allowed to file past and throw a small shovelful of dirt into the hole. When all turns were completed, several teachers joined in and finished filling the hole. Stomping hard, good old Frances then walked around and around the six-foot red maple tree, grimacing all the way. She resembled a one-person war party warming up for a raid.

Mr. Thomas, the band director and our youngest faculty member, then stepped forward and played "Taps" on his trumpet as the flag was raised. It was truly a "lump-in-the-throat" moment, and all were touched. We may occasionally neglect students, but we are faithfully patriotic.

My day was more hectic than usual with photographers taking pictures of various groups for the school yearbook. Each period resulted with segments of band students, student government members, or athletes leaving for the routine group pictures.

I didn't forget about the journal, but there never did seem to be an appropriate time for me to read it. After glancing through it, I tucked it into my canvas tote bag with the intention of reading it at home.

The day was so breath-takingly beautiful that I could

hardly wait to get outside and enjoy it fully. When I arrived home, it was four o'clock, as it usually is, unless I stop at the grocery store or library. While changing into sweats and tennis shoes, I hastily made supper decisions. In record time, I had assembled a meat loaf, quickly peeled some potatoes and carrots, and sprinkled the whole business with onion salt and lots of pepper. After popping it into the oven, I grabbed the dog leash and headed for Sasha's pen.

Sasha, my seven month old collie, has been much company for Dew and me since the kids left home. She is a golden-brown, full-sized, "Lassie-type" collie with a white blaze, ruff, and stockings. We picked her from a litter last spring when she was six weeks old. It was love at first sight.

Dew built a large exercise pen for her behind our barn, where she stays while we are gone. She can run in and out of the barn at will and opts to sleep there on a huge pile of straw during inclement weather.

Dew, Sasha, and I faithfully take a brisk three-mile walk down our winding country road every evening, except when it rains. For us, it is cardiovascular—our march against time; for Sasha it is pure joy.

As we walked that evening, Dew asked about the journal and was vaguely surprised that I had not read it yet. He had been most supportive in my decision to present it to Peggy Benson.

That night, propped up in bed with my usual reading pillows and my high-intensity reading lamp, I opened Johnny's journal:

Aug. 30-ABOUT ME

My name is Johnny Dale Benson. I am twelve years old. My birthday is March 24. I am in the seventh grade at Riley Middle School. Me and my mom live in a white house by the state forest. My grandma did live with us but she died last January. She had a heart attack. I don't have any brothers or sisters. My hobby is lizards.

Aug. 31- MY SUMMER VACATION

I liked my summer vacation. It was fun. I got to sleep alot and watch t.v. alot. I played in the forest every day. I waded in the creek. I caught lots of lizards. It was hot. Sometimes I rode my bike. Me and Mom ate lots of ice cream. She likes strawberry. I like chocolate chip best of all.

Sept. 1- SEPTEMBER IS-

September is a new month. It is not so hot in September. Grandma's birthday is September 19. If she did not die she would be 65. She is in heaven with my Grandpa Benson. I don't remember him. He died when I was only three. His name was Dale Eugene Benson. Grandma was Irene Clare Benson.

Sept. 2- SEVENTH GRADE IS-

Seventh grade is o.k. My teachers are nice. I don't like homework. Math is my best class. I made a hundred on my first math test. It was easy. I don't like gym because I'm not very good at running and playing ball. I hate it when they choose up teams and I don't get picked for a long time.

Sept. 3- MY WEEKEND PLANS

On the weekend I will try to find another lizard. Here's how you do it. You go into the forest and sit real still for a long time. Sit on a log and don't move. If it is warm and sunny when crickets chirp and bees buzz and flies buzz and grasshoppers jump, lizards will be out hunting. Listen for leaves rustling and watch. You might see a bright blue tail. Some have stripes. If you are quick you can catch one. It might bite you but they are not poisonous and it does not hurt very much. If you catch one don't be surprised if the tail drops off. But don't worry about it because they will grow a new one.

Sept. 7- MY HOBBY

My hobby is lizards. They are reptiles. They are cold blooded. I have seven. They make good pets. You can feed them insects or little brown pellets you buy at the pet shop. There are 3 thousand species of lizards. They are in size from one and a half inches to ten feet. Monitors are the big ones. There are no big ones around here. Some lizards live in water. Some glide or parachute from trees. They can run upsidedown across ceilings. Some live underground. Most have four legs and five toes on each foot. Some have no eyes. They lay eggs. They do not urinate. I have a chameleon. He can change colors to match his environment. I also have a gecko and five skinks. I would like to have a iguana.

Sept. 8- IF I HAD THREE WISHES-

If I had three wishes I would wish I had a father.
I wish I had a father.
I wish I had a father.

Sept. 9- TODAY IS-

Today is a rainy day. It is warm. I like rain. It washes everything and makes the world look cleaner. When it is summer I like to play outside in the rain. Rain makes the flowers and crops grow. Mushrooms grow real fast after a rain in the spring. I like to hunt mushrooms.

Sept. 10- WHEN I GROW UP-

When I grow up I want to work in a zoo. I will take care of all the lizards. I will tell children all about the lizards. I will let them touch some of them. They will be surprised how big monitors are. They are tropical.

Sept. 13- MY WEEKEND WAS-

My weekend was boring. It rained and I had to stay in the house. I wanted to go see a movie but Mom would not go because her friend came over. I do not like him. I don't like how he talks. I don't like how he looks at me. I wish he would stay away from our house.

Sept. 14- WHAT AMERICA MEANS TO ME

America means freedom to me. We can do what we want to do and don't have a king or nothing bossing us around. We like peace in our country. We vote for presidents and stuff. It means national holidays and our flag which is red, white, and blue. There are parades on holidays. I love America. We also have soldiers and navy men.

Sept. 15- MY FRIEND

I have lots of friends but not one special friend. The people in Grandma's church are friends. The teachers are friends. The police and bus drivers are friends. Friends should be nice to you. All the kids at school are friends except Fred. He is mean to me on the bus. He is 15.

Sept. 16- WHAT MAKES ME HAPPY

It makes me happy to lay in my bed at night and put my hand in my lizard box. I keep it by my bed. It has rocks and twigs in it. There is a lid with water in it. When I put my hand down there the lizards nibble my fingers with their sharp teeth a little at first but it does not hurt. They are used to me. When they know it is me they stop and lay down around my hand to sleep. They like the warm because lizards have poor circulation. Sometimes I go to sleep with my hand in their box. They like my hand. They like to lick my hand because of the saltiness. I like them.

Sept. 17- WHAT MAKES ME ANGRY

1. War and bombs
2. People being mean
3. Pollution
4. People who make fun of other people
5. Mean Dogs

Sept. 20- BLUE MAKES ME FEEL-

Blue is a good color. It is relaxing. It is a boy color. It is the color of sky and oceans. Some birds are blue. Morning glories are blue. I like blue. Some lizards have blue tails.

Sept. 21- A POEM

I have a secret
I have a mouth
I have a friend
His name is Ralph

Sept. 22- MY MOM

My mom is a good mom. She buys me things. She bought me a chameleon. It cost $5.00. She bought me a gecko. It cost $6.50. She takes me to the pet shop. She lets me pick the t.v. shows for us to watch. We go to the movies sometimes and to McDonalds. I like that. She is never mean to me. Sometimes she drinks too much and I don't like that. I am never going to drink.

Sept. 23- RALPH

I love Ralph. He is my favorite lizard. He is six inches long. He is a skink. I caught him in the state forest. He likes to ride on my shoulder and go everywhere I go. He does not like loud noises. I have had him for two years. I feed him food pellets and he takes drinks of water from a bottle. He likes to eat flies and crickets.

Sept. 24- YESTERDAY WAS-

Yesterday was good until he came over. I don't like him but Mom does. He brought lots of beer. They drink beer. They left in the car. I watched t.v. and went to bed. I wish he would stay away from our house. I opened all the windows when they left.

Sept. 27- FIVE THINGS I DON'T LIKE AND WHY

1. I don't like homework because I like to watch t.v..
2. I don't like people to drink beer because they talk stupid.
3. I don't like tornadoes because they destroy homes.
4. I don't like snakes because they eat lizards.
5. I don't like forest fires because they destroy animals homes.

Sept. 28- SOMETHING I LOST

One day I lost Ralph. He climbed out of his box and hid. I knew he was somewhere in my room. But I couldn't find him. Sometimes he climbs on my curtains. But he was not there. Once I saw him on the wall. He was hiding. There are lots of loose flies in the house. I knew he would not starve. I closed my door. I went to school. When I got home he was sunning himself on my bed. I was happy to find him.

Sept. 29- SOMEDAY I WILL

Someday I will grow up and be a man. I will own my grandpa's farm when I am twenty-one. I will still live in our house and Mom will still live there too. I will not let anyone come to my house that I don't like. Maybe I will get married and have three children. I will be a good father. I will take my children to the zoo. I will take them on walks in the forest and go on camping trips. I will teach them to play ball.

And that was all. I closed the journal gently as tears welled in my eyes. Oh, Johnny, I thought, you poor child. How you grieved over not having a father. What lonely days you must have spent at your isolated home by the state forest. Had your lizards been your only friends? Had the children made fun of you? What a sensitive, gentle boy you were and how unfairly life treated you. How sad that your short life is over, and you'll never have a chance to grow up and be the kind of father that you deserved to have.

Putting the journal aside and extinguishing the light, I lay waiting for sleep and thought of our own happy, suntanned children and how rich and full their childhoods had been. I recalled camping trips in the mountains and wonderful summer vacations at the seashore. Little League games, piano lessons, 4-H fairs, band, and school athletics had all been taken for granted. Johnny had had so little in his short lifetime.

At school the next morning, I headed for Roxie's room with the journal. I needed her opinion about giving it to Peggy Benson. Although most of it echoed a sweet, childish innocence, I was concerned about the part expressing his disdain for his mother's drinking. The last thing I wanted was to sadden her or add to her guilt.

When I reached her room, a substitute teacher met me and explained that Roxie was attending the funeral of a great aunt but would be back on Wednesday. I decided to wait until then to make any more decisions about the journal.

Back in my own room, I settled into my swivel desk chair and reread the journal entries. Soon my students began clamoring into the room with the usual: "Know what, Mrs. Brown? Know what?" I slid the journal into my desk drawer.

As I went through my daily routine, something kept bothering me about the journal. I couldn't quite put a handle on it, but it kept gnawing at me, haunting me from the fringes of my memory. Call it woman's intuition, insight, or E.S.P.; but it was there and was vaguely unsettling. In some obscure way, I knew that something was amiss. I needed to talk to Roxie or Dew to confirm the growing fear within me . . . the fear that something was terribly wrong.

During my sixth period prep, I once more read the entries and the words almost leaped out at me: "I don't like snakes because they eat lizards." Johnny KNEW that snakes were enemies of lizards. Why then Johnny, I thought, did you bring a snake into your room and jeopardize your beloved lizards?

Unless Johnny DIDN'T bring the snake into the house! Which meant . . . that someone else must have put the poisonous snake in his room. Lightbulbs began flashing inside my head, and bells began ringing in my ears. What had actually happened? Who would have wanted to hurt Johnny? Did someone want Johnny dead? Was he murdered? Was there any kind of investigation? Who would benefit from his death? I knew the implications were enormous. The very thought gave me the willies and sent shivers up my spine.

I desperately needed to talk and share my newborn apprehension with someone. I needed Roxie, but she was not due back until the next day. I couldn't bear to wait and felt like someone would pull my tongue out, if I didn't share my revelation.

Quickly, I made my way to the copy machine and made copies of the pages for Roxie. Since I had been trained at college to always defer to administrators, I headed resolutely to Dr. Fitzbaum's office with my damning evidence of foul play, feeling like a senior Nancy Drew ready to bust a case.

Franny Bumpus was typing away while simultaneously talking into a phone wedged between her ear and shoulder. She was wearing a hot-pink jumpsuit with a pineapple brooch at her throat and a brightly colored scarf tied about her waist. Her shoes were lime-green, pink, and yellow canvas platforms. A rhinestone-studded fuschia headband shone through her frizzy bleached hair. Large enameled fruit collections swung from each ear. I'm sure she was making some sort of fashion statement, but I was not literate enough to interpret it. Maybe, I thought, it was "Jamaica Day" or "Calypso Dancers Week."

When I indicated a desire to speak to the good doctor, Franny signified that he was available, and that I should go on back to his office. Easing around the counter, I saw three boys sitting on a vinyl couch. No doubt they were badasses serving detention time.

In dire need of haircuts, they all wore black T-shirts bearing symbols of rock groups and had cheap gold crosses dangling from tarnished chains around their necks. Holes dotted their dirty jeans. All wore scruffy cowboy boots and had red bandannas tied around their heads. I wondered if these guys shopped at a "Punks R Us" store. Obviously, they couldn't risk being original. Undoubtedly, these boys had attitude problems, confirmed by their slouching demeanor and smirking expressions. Their eyes were glued to the voluptuous secretary; I concluded that Franny Bumpus was probably the star of many adolescent dreams.

Dr. Fitzbaum was seated at his desk with a phone pressed to his ear. He nodded amicably towards a chair indicating that I should be seated. The walls of his office held several framed degrees and certificates, as well as various plaques and civic awards. Family portraits graced his desktop, and Indiana Hoosiers basketball memorabilia dotted the remaining spaces. His only passion, Dr. Fitzbaum had developed an almost-perverse love for I.U. Being an I.U. graduate and a Hoosiers fan myself, it was comforting to know we shared a common interest.

As I waited for him to wind up his perfunctory conversation, I noticed for the first time how his thin hair, parted on the side, somewhat resembled an EKG wave. I waited patiently and wondered idly if Dr. Fitzbaum knew he suffered from denture breath. I guessed his age to be somewhere in his late fifties. Finally he settled the telephone into its cradle, folded his hands on his desk, and met my eyes.

"And what can I do for you, Mrs. Brown?"

"Dr. Fitzbaum, Did anyone investigate Johnny Benson's death?"

"Well, I suppose the sheriff's department looked everything over. Why do you ask?"

"I know you'll probably think I'm crazy, but I suspect foul play." I whipped out the journal. "My students write daily in their journals and I just read Johnny's. He knew that snakes would kill lizards and he LOVED lizards. He kept some in a box by his bed. There's no way he would have brought a snake near his pet lizards!" I continued with my jolting perceptions.

Indulgently, he listened and nodded perfunctorily. Clearly, he thought I was insane or having some kind of a mid-life crisis. Leveling his gaze at me, he spoke kindly and deliberately.

"Mrs. Brown, I do appreciate your concern about Johnny." His voice was gentle. "We all feel badly for him and for his family. It was a poor home situation. But nobody would hurt that boy. He was a child and children don't always use good judgment; he made a mistake and paid a dear price."

"But Johnny was a bright boy," I pleaded. "He knew all about reptiles; he studied them. I'm sure he knew about poisonous snakes. Don't you think we should at least talk to the sheriff and show the journal to him?"

"I'll tell you what I'll do, Mrs. Brown." He smiled and spoke glibly. "You leave the journal with me and I'll read it and think about it. If I think there is the slightest bit of evidence to support your theory, I will personally call the sheriff." He paused thoughtfully. "Until then, I think it best if you did not speak of this matter to anyone. You know how fast rumors spread in small towns. We wouldn't want the sheriff's department to feel that we question their judgment. And we certainly don't want to further upset the family; Heaven knows they've been through enough." I sank deeper into my chair and bit my lower lip for restraint.

Then he imparted philosophically: "This has been difficult for you, I realize. A student's death is always traumatic. Why don't you just take a couple of days off and rest?" Another smile. "Then when you come back to school, you'll feel much better about everything."

He was patronizing me and I knew it; but being compliant by nature, I thanked him for his time and left Johnny's journal on his desk. That was my first mistake.

Chapter Four

As I worked through my seventh period class, I felt as if I were in the middle of a bad dream . . . a dream in which I was standing in the midst of a jeering mob, who were all laughing at me for being so absurd. My vivid imagination was working overtime, and doubts and suspicions piled up like wind-blown leaves against a country fence row.

On the way home, I kept hearing Johnny's line: "I don't like snakes, because they eat lizards." I was truly convinced by then that he had NOT brought the deadly snake into his bedroom—the room where he loved to lie in bed with his hand in his lizard box as he drifted into sleep. Who then . . . and why?

When I heard the crunching of tires as Dew's red pickup truck pulled into our gravel driveway, I was in full flight to meet him. "Oh, Dew," I blurted, "I think someone murdered Johnny Benson, and no one thinks so but me!" By then I was so wired that it's a wonder all my hair wasn't standing straight up on end.

Climbing down from his truck, Dew set his book bag down. "Oh . . . my God," he murmured and opened his arms to me. I rushed to him and nestled against his chest; it always offered refuge to me in times of turmoil. Dew is almost six feet tall and his chest is just the perfect height for my face.

Even at forty-seven, Dew is still solid and fit. His dark hair and skin are thought to be remnants of some Native American heritage. His prodigious love of nature and expert hunting skills confirm those considerations.

We attended the same schools and have been in love since we were teenagers. After twenty-five years of marriage, we are still lovers and best friends. Acquaintances sometimes comment about our being together so much, but I can't think of anyone with whom I would rather spend time. We make each other laugh and have grown together so indelibly that sometimes I mistakenly recall his adventures and dreams as my own. We are mated for life . . . like Canadian geese.

"It's in his journal—I just know—someone PLANTED that snake in his room. They WANTED it to bite him. He would NEVER have put a snake where it could get to his lizards!" I poured out all my suspicions and fears with great gulps.

"Relax, Margo," he said calmly as he held me away at arm's length and looked deeply into my eyes. "Think what you're saying! Be sure that you're not jumping to conclusions. If you're wrong; innocent people could be hurt. His mother has already suffered so much."

"But, Dew, I just feel it," I pleaded. "Something is terribly wrong. Don't you understand? Nobody has ever stood up for that little boy. I'm NOT going to let him down this time."

"I want to read the journal," Dew said calmly. He was well acquainted with my relentless determination and knew that I would never give up easily.

"I left it with Dr. Fitzbaum . . . but, wait, I made copies of the pages for Roxie to read; I'll bring them home tomorrow."

As we walked with Sasha that evening, I struggled to recall everything I could about Johnny's journal. Later, as we prepared spaghetti and salad for supper, I felt gratified that I had shared my feelings with him. Burdens are always lighter when shared with a friend . . . someone said that.

The next morning Roxie returned, and without hesitation I threw discretion to the wind and told her everything that had transpired during her absence. She took the copies of the pages to class with her and promised to read them at her earliest convenience.

During lunch we didn't speak of the matter due to the presence of our colleagues, but she gave me a knowing look, and I knew she had read the pages and was in agreement with me. As soon as our sixth-period prep began, she came bursting into my room.

"I think you're on to something," she said concretely. "But that one sentence isn't enough evidence. We need to find out more about Johnny and the circumstances of his death."

"What would Agatha Christie do?" I quipped. Roxie had read every one of her mystery novels.

"Probably a lot of questioning and surveillance," she replied matter-of-factly. "But you'd better wait until Dr. Fitzbaum reads it and talks to you."

"Right," I said and told myself to be patient and wait upon the powers that be. But I knew it would be difficult. I have a tendency to be impetuous and rush into matters, often regretting later that I had not been more cautious.

When I went to Dr. Fitzbaum's office the next morning, anxious to hear his verdict, he was involved in a hearing and had asked not be disturbed. On Friday, Franny informed me that he was at a regional principals' meeting and would be out of the office all day. When I

asked if he had left any messages for me, she gave a negative reply without glancing up from her typing. I would
have to wait until Monday to discuss the matter with him.

As I returned to my classroom, three questions were
crowding my mind: Had Dr. Fitzbaum been too busy
to read the journal? Had he read it and deemed it so unimportant that he had not even bothered to reply? Was
Dr. Fitzbaum purposely avoiding me? The last one
troubled me.

Time has a way of deadening impulses and soothing
jangled nerves. As the day wore on, I began to doubt my
own intuitions. Maybe I WAS overreacting to a little
boy's careless words. Maybe it really DID happen just as
it had been reported. Surely if he thought it amounted
to anything, Dr. Fitzbaum would have gotten in touch
with me. Maybe I truly WAS having a mid-life crisis. As
my students filed out, I loaded my tote bag and headed
for home.

Both Leigh and Will have birthdays in October and
were coming home to celebrate with us on the weekend.
They were due home by six o'clock, so I dropped by the
local pizzeria and picked up two large combination pizzas
and an order of breadsticks with cheese sauce. I never
cook on Fridays; it is one of my foibles.

Dew and I were regular Friday-night pizza patrons, and
I usually picked up a rental movie. Since we had purchased a big-screen T.V. for Christmas the year before,
we enjoyed home movies almost as much as going to the
theater, and it was a heck of a lot cheaper. With kids in
college, it was a worthy consideration.

It was interesting how going off to school had matured
our children and increased their appreciation of family and
home. They didn't come home very often, but when
they did, we strived for quality time with them.

On Saturday, Leigh and I spent the day shopping for birthday gifts at the mall, where we have shared some of our finest moments. Inheriting her father's dark features and quiet ways, she is in many ways more his child then mine. However, as with Dew and me, our personalities compliment one another, and we have always enjoyed a good relationship. As her willowy body modeled clothes, I invariably wanted to buy them all for her. Indelible bonding between mothers and daughters that once took place around quilting frames, now occurs in shopping malls all over America.

The blond Will, on the other hand, is mine. Not quite as tall as his father, his fair complexion and sturdy frame come from my people. Impetuous and good-humored, his easy smile and quick wit have made him popular among his peers.

Both children are serious students and toiling earnestly towards medical professions. Their dedication and self-discipline at times astound their father and me, as we recall no similar intensity during our college years. We are proud parents, and rightly so, of these two handsome children who are reaching so high—these two who sprang from our loins.

Dew and Will spent the day hunting quail, those elusive, woodsy little birds with meat that qualifies as the sweetest of all of God's creatures. One of their favorite pastimes, they always anticipated quail season with great eagerness.

When Leigh and I arrived home, arms laden with new clothes, the victorious hunters—adept at their skill, had already started supper. Tiny quail breasts were sizzling in my electric skillet. Although it takes several birds to make a meal, this seasonal treat of tender white meat is delectable and fit for a king's table.

While Dew was tending to the main course, Will was

struggling with a biscuit recipe on the back of a Bisquick box. Golden ears of corn were washed and ready to drop into steaming water. It was a memorable meal—a man's meal. As we savored the supper and exchanged anecdotes of our day's adventures, I reveled in the warmth of family and love.

After church on Sunday, all the aunts, uncles, and cousins arrived for our annual birthday-wiener roast. The day was cool enough to make the big bonfire plausible. There were about twenty or so of us to enjoy what was probably the last picnic of the season. Baked beans, potato salad, chips, and birthday cake rounded out the menu with lots of coffee and hot chocolate. Sasha showed off by leaping into the air and catching the frisbee . . . her newest trick.

After the relatives left and the mess was cleaned up, we helped the kids load their cars. It was always mandatory that each carried back a zip-locked bag of homemade chocolate chip cookies, some fresh fruit, and a case of soda pop. They had two and three-hour drives back to their respective universities, so we insisted upon an early departure time and a reassuring phone call as soon as they landed. Parents forever, I guess. Probably when I'm ninety-years old, and they come to visit me at "The Home," I'll ask them to call and let me know they got home safely. Suggesting that if they didn't, I'd go zooming over in my wheelchair to rescue them like the Lone Ranger.

As we walked Sasha that evening, we spoke for the first time that weekend of the Johnny Benson case. Admittedly, I had lost some of my zeal for the topic, but was still anxious to speak to my superior.

On Monday morning, I tripped up to the front office, first thing on my agenda. Franny relayed that Dr.

Fitzbaum was on the phone and had asked not to be disturbed; I should come back during my prep period . . . another put-off. I began to wonder if he was ever going to talk to me.

However, it was not uncommon to be kept waiting by an administrator. Sometimes it took weeks to receive word on a simple request, such as approval for a purchase or a student activity. And this was indeed a weighty matter. I decided to be patient.

When Roxie came to my room later that day, she was all smiles. "Well, what did the good doctor think about the journal?" she asked.

"I haven't been able to talk to him yet. He's either been out of town or tied up with someone ever since I gave it to him. It will probably be sixth period today before I can talk to him." I was weary with waiting.

"I saw Burley Haggard going into his office just after lunch today. They closed the door and I figured they were talking about it."

That settled it in my mind. He must have thought it valid enough to discuss with the sheriff. At once and without warning, my sleuthing genes activated again, renewing my confidence that my hunch was right on target. I could hardly wait for sixth period to arrive. Teachers love to be right; it's some kind of genetic factor.

When I reached the front office, Franny smiled and said amiably, "Go on back, Margo, Dr. F. is waiting for you." I loved the way she called him "Dr. F." and wondered only slightly what the kids would do with that bit of information. I nodded appreciatively as I moved around the counter and through the doorway to Leo's office.

Sitting comfortably at his large oak desk, Dr. Fitzbaum smiled and said easily, "How are you today, Mrs. Brown?"

"Fine, thank you."

"Have a seat, please." I sat.

"Did you have a nice weekend?"

I smiled and nodded. "A busy one; the kids were both home for their birthdays. We always have a family get-to-gether."

"That's nice," he said, smiling in earnest. "They sure do grow up fast, don't they?"

I nodded again and wondered if he was ever going to get to the point of my visit.

He cleared his throat and tapped his pencil. "About the Benson boy's writing, Mrs. Brown." He paused. "After carefully reading it, I have decided that we have no reason to question the decisions and judgements of the boy's mother or the sheriff's department."

"But Johnny KNEW that snakes would kill his lizards!" I blurted as I scooted to the edge of my chair.

He continued patiently, "Agreeably, he may have known that snakes might be poisonous or that they might kill his lizards. But kids are like that. Children know that playing with matches causes fires, but they do it anyway. That's why children need supervision. And sadly, Johnny Benson had very little supervision." His voice rang with condescension.

"Dr. Fitzbaum, I just don't feel right about it," I commented lamely. I had no more ammunition and I knew it.

"Try to forget about it, Mrs. Brown. Let it go and get on with your year. We can't take responsibility for our students' home lives." He spoke with finality; he had settled the issue. He folded his hands on his desk and stared at me. It was my cue to leave.

"I'll try," I sighed. And then almost as an afterthought, I asked, "Could I please have the journal back? I thought his mother might enjoy keeping it."

He looked thoughtful and took a deep breath, exhaling slowly. He then replied cautiously, "That would be a nice gesture. However, I left it at home. I'll try to remember to bring it for you." His lips widened into a peaceful smile.

I thought about the great writer, Ernest Hemingway, and his "built-in, shock-proof shit detector" and sorely wished that I had one. If I had, I'm sure it would have been buzzing and flashing red lights right then.

Early the next morning, Roxie popped into my classroom carrying a steaming mug of coffee. It read: "IF MAMA AIN'T HAPPY—AIN'T NOBODY HAPPY." Her lowest set of earrings were three-inch skeletons with hinged body parts that jiggled as she walked.

As she listened intently, I reiterated the dreary dialogue with Dr. Fitzbaum during our latest encounter. I emphasized his condescending tone. She recognized the defeat in my voice.

"Actually, I'm surprised he didn't give me a drink of water, pat me on the head, and send me off to bed."

"You aren't going to give up that easily, are you?"

"Of course not, I just haven't thought it out yet. Dew read the copies of the journal pages. He thinks we're on shaky ground. What do you propose?"

Her face lit up. "Let's go talk to Peggy Benson," she said impishly.

"Under what pretense? We can't very well just say, 'Peggy, we think Johnny was murdered. Did you do it?'"

"Let's tell her we want to adopt Johnny's lizards for the junior-high science lab, and all the students will enjoy them. She'll buy it." Her eyes sparkled with adventure.

"I love it!" I said excitedly. "And while we're there, we'll look around. Maybe she'll show us Johnny's room and tell us about the snake."

Our plans were finalized. A surge of excitement washed over me the next evening as Roxie and I, like Sherlock Holmes and Dr. Watson, drove through desolate coal-mined land that fringed the state forest. We were on our way to Peggy Benson's house . . . the scene of the heinous crime.

Chapter Four

After driving through miles of farms and wooded areas, we traveled on a dirt road used mainly by coal trucks. Land that had once been fertile farm ground and rolling wooded homesites had been ravaged by strip-mining and had taken on the stark appearance of a moonscape. Huge pits and gashes in the earth were lined with roadways for enormous earth-moving machines. Once-proud farmers and landowners had succumbed to the proffered greenery of the land rapists.

After several miles of desolation, we approached the pristine state forest. In 1942, over two thousand acres of forest had been set aside by some prudent and insightful lawmakers. Due to the varied topography of both hilly uplands and low bottomland spanning to the river, a wide variety of plant and animal life could be observed. In the center of the forest was a watchtower, used by fire patrols during dry weather. Hiking and bridle trails winding through the forest invited a few horse lovers and avid birdwatchers.

Every spring, the local scout troops held their annual camp-outs on the fringes of the state acreage. Other than those few interlopers, the forest was basically a wildlife preserve. It was a haven for white-tailed deer, foxes, coyote, rabbits, squirrels, woodchucks, raccoon, chipmunks, skunks, opossum, and weasels. Mink, beaver, and musk-rats dwelt along the creeks that threaded through the woods. Once a year, anxious hunters were allowed to enter and hunt wild turkeys and deer. Licenses were carefully scrutinized and game limits were adamantly enforced by brown-clad conservation officers.

A few scattered homes sat along the road that divided the coal-mine property and the state forest. We passed the austere Calvary Baptist Church, where Johnny's funeral had been held. It was a small frame structure with neither steeple nor stained-glass windows. An old cemetery lay behind it, with many tombstones in disrepair —either from age or vandalism.

We were approximately one-quarter of a mile from the Benson home at that point. According to Roxie, the nearest home on the other side of Peggy's house was at least that far and maybe farther. As we pulled into Peggy Benson's gravel driveway, I was overwhelmed at the isolation of the area. What a lonely place for a boy to grow up!

Behind the house, tall trees stood like environmental sentinels, and I was not sure where the forest started and the yard ended. The house was a typical one-story, white frame home with a porch spanning the front. A slatted porch swing hung on one end, and a boy's red bicycle leaned against the house on the other end. Four concrete steps were centered in front, and a wooden railing ran around the porch connecting the four posts that supported the roof.

A small, unattached garage sat beside the house with its doors open exposing Peggy Benson's car. The conservative, gray Buick Skylark looked to be three or four years old.

On the clothesline behind the house, an assortment of Peggy's clothes still hung, even though it was almost dark. I wondered what she had done with Johnny's clothes that never had seemed to fit him. The thought made me ache.

As we crossed the front porch, Peggy opened the door and greeted us. We had called and asked if we could come out and visit her, so we were expected. She was wearing faded, navy-blue sweat pants and an oversized, pink blouse which she had left hanging on the outside. Her tennis shoes were the cheap kind and were bright turquoise-blue. She wore no make-up and no jewelry. Her reddish-brown hair still hung limply about her shoulders, but she looked much better than she had at our first meeting.

As she led us into the living room, I noticed that the layout of rooms was exactly like my grandparents' home when I was a child. An archway divided the living and dining rooms, which were exactly the same size. Standing in the doorway, a brick fireplace centered the right side of the living room with a small window on each side. Directly behind the dining room was a small kitchen, which led out to a covered back porch. The door leading to the basement was also in the kitchen. On the left side of these three rooms were two bedrooms with a bathroom in the middle. In order to get to the bathroom, one had to go through somebody's bedroom.

Slightly faded floral wallpaper covered the walls. The carpet was celery-green and had a sculptured texture. Tiny lint particles suggested that it had not been vacuumed for a few days.

Although the furniture was slightly worn, it appeared comfortable with crocheted doilies covering all available backs and arms. Two planters sat on a coffee table and a small angel was attached to one of them; I recalled seeing them at the funeral home. Although Peggy's housekeeping was not spotless, it was decent. Stacks of movie magazines were piled haphazardly on both end-tables. An assortment of cellophane-wrapped candies filled a glass candy dish.

On top of the television sat a portrait of an elderly couple—surely Dale and Irene Benson. They looked pleasant and amazingly alike with gray hair and silver-rimmed glasses. Beside it was a picture of Johnny as a toddler in a blue sailorsuit. His expression was one of vague wonder, as if unaccustomed to the happy world of photography. A religious picture hung on one wall between gilded sconces filled with plastic flowers.

Peggy invited us to sit down, so Roxie and I settled onto the floral couch. Peggy sat in an over-stuffed chair facing us. I began the conversation.

"How are you doing, Peggy? We know this has been very hard for you." My voice was gentle and sincere.

"Pretty good, you know everyone says 'Life goes on.' I just have to get over it." She was very composed.

"Have you seen the tree planted in Johnny's memory at the school?"

"Yeah, that was really nice. Oh . . . by the way, I'm glad you came. I found a book in Johnny's room that should go back to the school library. Maybe you could take it back for me."

At this juncture she got up, went into the back bedroom, and returned with a book in her hands. When she handed it to me, I saw that it was P. Stanley Carlson's *The Interesting World of Lizards*. I took it and assured her that I would see that it got back to school.

Roxie noticed the book and took advantage of the moment: "Ms. Benson, one of the reasons for our being here was to ask you about Johnny's lizards."

She smiled and nodded. "He just loved them; I always thought it was kind of silly, but boys have to have something to play with, you know." She seemed remarkably detached.

Continuing, Roxie added, "We were wondering if you would like to donate them for the school science lab. We would keep them in our terrarium; the kids would love them."

Peggy looked thoughtful, then spoke quickly, "I already turned some of them loose . . . the ones he caught in the forest. I still have the two that I bought for him. I was afraid they'd die in the forest. I was going to take them back to the pet store and see if they wanted them, but you can take them if you want them." She smiled at the idea.

"Great!" Roxie said as if to reassure her that she had done the right thing. "Johnny would be pleased to know that the other children were enjoying his lizards. We'll take good care of them."

Feeling that our visit was nearing its end, I abruptly changed the subject: "You know, my grandparents' home was just like this house! I'll bet you have two bedrooms with a bath in the middle . . . and a door to the basement in kitchen."

Taken back, Peggy stated, "Well, that's exactly right. Would you like to see the house? I'll show you."

"We'd love to!" I answered quickly and felt no shame at all. "Why don't we just go with you to get Johnny's lizards . . . he told me he kept them by his bed."

At that, we got up and shamelessly followed Peggy through the dining room and into the doorway of Johnny's room. By today's standards, it was a large bedroom. A single bed with a faded cowboy-bedspread stood near one wall. Over his bed was a small poster bearing the words: FRIENDS DON'T LET FRIENDS DRIVE DRUNK. One window was near the head of the bed and another by the foot of the bed. The bedside table was cluttered with comic books and a small, electric alarm clock. The only other piece of furniture in the room was an old, scarred bureau with six drawers. The attached mirror displayed a bumper sticker which read: SAY NO TO DRUGS. All sixth graders at Riley Middle School received such literature as part of the school's alcohol and drug-awareness program.

Johnny's seventh-grade school picture sat in a cardboard frame on top of the bureau. Shaggy, light brown hair was barely out of his eyes. His skin was clear and his expression was somewhat wistful. The neck opening of his faded, blue sweatshirt was stretched wide, revealing a dingy-white T-shirt. Odds and ends of typical boy-junk littered the bureau top: a flashlight, a small pocketknife, a compass, baseball cards, several plastic buttons, and ballpoint pens.

Two boxes sat on the floor along the wall opposite of his bed—between the door and the bureau. One was a large, wooden box that surely had been built as a toybox. It seemed to be mostly full of junk and old boots, but I did see a box of Lincoln Logs and a dented Tonka dump truck. The other box was smaller and made of heavy cardboard; it had a fitted screen top. A small catching-net lay on top of the screen. On the side of the box in black printed letters were the words: Lizard City.

"Here we are," Peggy said easily as she lifted the screened lid from the lizard box. Several rocks and branched sticks provided climbing surfaces for the citizens of Lizard City. What resembled a lid from a mayonnaise jar created the city pool. The first thing that I noticed about the lizards was that their tails were twice as long as their bodies. We all dropped to our knees for a better view of the little reptiles.

"The littlest one is the chameleon—he can change colors," Peggy imparted with authority. "The one with the funny feet is a gecko . . . he can climb up a mirror."

As we watched the lizards, I was amazed by their soft,

pliable, almost velvety appearance. Nothing slimy here, I thought. The toes of the gecko were wide, flat, and extremely flexible. Both lizards had eyes that were large and capable of revolving independently. How convenient if teachers could do that! Instead of eyelids, they seemed to have transparent shields that covered their eyes . . . so clear and thin that they were hardly noticeable. Occasionally, a long, fleshy tongue ran out and back in. They seemed totally undaunted by our presence.

"Johnny told me that he liked to go to sleep with his hand in the lizard box," I offered, hoping to encourage Peggy to talk. "Did they not ever climb out?"

"Sometimes they did, but he just put them back in when he woke up. He played with them on his bed a lot, especially one. He had one so tame he'd ride his shoulder all day."

"Ah . . . Ralph!" I added with a smile, "We met Ralph at school."

"I told him he might get in trouble if he took him to school, but he said no one cared; teachers sure are a lot nicer now than when I was in school," Peggy laughed.

"It was terrible about the snake," I offered in a soft tone. "Did he play with snakes much?"

"I didn't know that he ever did. Me and Mom were always scared of snakes," Peggy confided. "It must have been the first time he messed with snakes; he knew if he told me I wouldn't like it, so he didn't tell me."

"Do you think he put the snake in the lizard box?" I queried. "Was the box by his bed that morning?"

"Yeah, I guess he did. The box was right there by the side of his bed like it always was in the morning. The lid was off, and he had been bit on his left arm . . . right about here," Peggy said as she pointed to her left arm midway between her hand and her elbow.

She continued, "His alarm clock always goes off at seven. I just kept hearing it ringing that morning and wondered why he didn't shut it off. When I came in here to tell him to get up for school, I couldn't wake him up. I thought he was in a coma or something. I got so scared . . . I called Sonny Ray and he came right over." She stopped and got teary-eyed.

"You don't have to talk about it," I said with true sympathy and patted her hand.

Peggy bit her lower lip and closed her eyes momentarily. Then she stated adamantly: "No, I have to get over it; that's what everyone says. Sonny Ray shot the snake and carried it out. He said it was in the lizard box. He called his dad and the funeral home and everything for me. I guess I was sorta in shock."

Closing her eyes, she took a deep breath and exhaled slowly. Then she continued, "The preacher said God probably wanted Johnny to be in Heaven with his Grandma and Grandpa, and I should accept that and try to be happy." I was completely appalled at the logic.

"You need to keep busy, Peggy; do you have a job?" I said in my Dear Abby mood.

"No, I get disability," she said as she brushed the hair from her eyes. "Working makes me too nervous, but I may help out at the senior citizen center. They have a van and take senior citizens shopping and out to eat. My aunts go there, and they told me that younger people sometimes go along and help the elderly. They talked to the people in charge, and they want me to start soon. I'm thinking about it."

Roxie entered, "Sounds like a great idea, and it would get you out once in a while."

"I might, but. . ." She giggled shyly, "I might be getting married."

"Well, congratulations!" I replied quickly, "Who is the lucky man?" Hope springs eternal . . .

Her smile faded. "Well, I really can't say, yet. You see, he used to go with this other woman, and she don't know about us. He's trying to break up with her, so we can get married, but he has to do it slowly. He said she might kill herself if he broke up with her real quick-like. He told me to just be patient." I wondered who the jackass was.

I had to ask: "Peggy, were you at home the evening before Johnny died?"

She answered slowly, "Yeah, we ate supper and then me and my boyfriend went for a drive."

I was pushing my luck and I knew it, but I pressed on: "What time did you get home?"

"Probably around one o'clock or so . . . I don't remember for sure."

"Did you look in on Johnny when you got home?"

"No . . . he just watches T.V. and goes on to bed when I'm gone. I knew he'd be asleep. I just went on to bed."

"Did Johnny keep the doors locked when he was home alone?"

"Just the front one. I always came in the back door when I came home, and then I locked it. He was never afraid. There's never anyone out this way at night."

"Did Johnny like your boyfriend?" Nosy me.

"I guess Johnny was jealous that I liked someone besides him . . . you know how kids are." She brushed it off as if it were nothing.

"Did Johnny ever have friends over to play?" Roxie inquired.

"No . . . we live so far out here. There's no kids close. He just had friends at school." She didn't have a clue.

"Do you know about a boy named Fred? Johnny said something about him being mean to him on the bus," I asked.

"He never told me nothing about that," she replied off-handedly.

"Oh, well," I offered, "it was probably nothing, you

know how boys are."

At that, we thanked Peggy Benson for allowing us to visit. We gathered up the lizard box, catching net, and food pellets and headed back to the living room. She walked us to the door and thanked us for taking the library book back for her. We wished her luck with her boyfriend and she smiled pleasantly.

As we drove home, Roxie and I discussed our interview with Peggy. We decided that she was not a suspect. Although she appeared detached and was probably a poor parent, she surely did not kill her child. Who then? It would have been so easy for someone to enter the house and plant the snake near Johnny during the night . . . especially if they knew he was home alone. The forest provided perfect coverage for someone to slip into the unlocked back door. We knew we had to find out who the elusive boyfriend was . . . a little surveillance seemed to be in order.

And we definitely had to ask more questions: Who was Fred? And what about Johnny's statement in the journal referring to his owning the farm when he was twenty-one? Who owned it now? We recalled the two aunts from the funeral home and planned to visit them next. Maybe they could give us the name of the boyfriend . . . and maybe a motive.

Teachers love fall break. At one time, it was referred to as "Teachers'-Institute Days," and teachers were required to attend professional meetings. During the past few years, a four-day weekend evolved as a permanent part of the school calendar. Meetings became optional, as teachers and students alike welcomed the freedom from the classroom during the glorious days of October. Happy campers hauled their trailers out for one last outing before winterizing them.

Dew had been after me to take a canoe trip with him,

so on Thursday afternoon we headed for the water. A large creek flowed within a quarter mile of our house. At places, it was almost thirty feet wide. Trees lined the banks offering shade and privacy.

We hauled our canoe to the launching point and then drove to the jumping-off point where the creek flowed into the murky river. Parking the truck there, we were then picked up by Dew's brother Tice and driven back to the waiting canoe to launch our watery journey.

It was relaxing to glide silently like Indians along the winding stream on that golden October day. Startled deer sprang away from the water's edge as we furtively approached. Several noisy ducks rose languidly, only to settle further downstream to be disturbed by us once more. A row of sleepy turtles basking in rays of dappled sunshine tumbled off a water-soaked log as we came into view. We identified prints of elusive raccoons along the muddy banks, and one wary beaver slapped his tail on the water as a warning to his peers and a protest to our intrusion.

We had taken cold drinks and snacks and enjoyed respite under the overhanging rocky ledges. In several places, foamy water rushed over rocks; shooting the rapids was brief, but exhilarating. The day was crisp and breath-takingly beautiful—just cool enough to warrant jackets.

As we floated lazily along under the spectacular canopy of tree-borne fire, we spoke of our children, our jobs, and life in general. Neither of us wanted to discuss anything that might dampen our soaring spirits.

After three hours, we arrived at our juncture and reluctantly loaded our craft into the waiting truck. As we drove home, we agreed that memories such as that golden afternoon would sustain us in our old age.

That evening as I slid an iron skillet full of barbecued chicken and a pan of potato wedges into the waiting oven, we discussed the Benson case. As I prepared salad, Dew heard all the details of our visit. He was supportive, but thought maybe I had been too inquisitive. (He's a staunch believer in privacy, whereas I'm not.) We carried our supper out to the picnic table on the deck and noticed how quickly dusk had settled upon us.

On Friday morning, I awoke sneezing and hosting an itchy throat . . . my first cold of the season. Overnight, a cold front had moved in, and the day was gray and rainy. The wind was gusty and was doing quite a job on the leaves. We were glad we had enjoyed Thursday, because the rest of our four-day weekend was predicted to be wet and gloomy.

When suffering a cold, I have a tendency to go into hibernation. I slept in as late as I could manage. Then, following an old family tradition, I chopped vegetables and made a huge pot of nourishing homemade soup— our trusted remedy for the common cold.

Wrapped warmly in a bathrobe, I stayed in all day Friday and Saturday and ate, slept, and watched old movies. I also made plans to visit all of Johnny Benson's aunts on Sunday afternoon: the two older ladies that I had seen at the funeral home . . . and Franny Bumpus. And I had fabricated a perfectly good reason to question them.

Chapter Six

By Sunday afternoon, I had once more declared victory over the common cold and wondered idly if I should try to patent my soup remedy. Although I was still sniffling a bit, my energy level had returned to normal, and I was anxious to get on with my interviews. After tucking a white turtleneck into my jeans, I pulled on an oversized ski sweater. While it was true that layering did keep one warmer, no one ever mentioned that it also helped hide a multitude of shapeless bodies. Not wanting to take any chances with wet feet, I opted for my trusty, old high-topped Reeboks and thick socks.

At the last minute, I checked into a mirror, decided that my cropped hair didn't look so hot, and covered it with my denim fisherman's hat. At that, I swung the leather strap of my purse over my shoulder and picked up my wire-bound notebook. Easing the car out of the garage, I then headed for Pleasantville, Riley County's biggest town.

Most of the leaves had been forced to their final resting places by the elements. Mounds of sodden leaves were piled sadly along the curbs, waiting to be scooped away by the town's faithful street-sweeper crews. The rain had let up, but the day was chilly and dismal with the wind coming in fitful gusts.

Irene Benson's sisters, Nora and Sadie Stanniger, had been most receptive when I asked to visit them. According to Roxie, the maiden sisters were products of Riley County and had lived together in the same house all of their lives. Both retired now, Nora had worked for forty years at the Pleasantville Public Library and had been as much a fixture there as the bookshelves themselves. Sadie had worked almost as long at the telephone company.

They had cared for their aging parents in a sterling display of daughterly affection and then took over the homeplace at their demise. A brother, Lewis, had been killed in Germany during World War II as a young man. Only Irene had married and had children.

Pleasantville's Main Street resembled the setting of a 1940's movie. Maple trees lined the streets and quaint turn-of-the-century stores sat proudly against brick sidewalks. Being the county seat, the courthouse was the major landmark. The three-story brick structure boasted a domed roof with a stained-glass window. Aged pine trees, those scarred and silent witnesses of the past, swayed in rhythm with the gusty afternoon breezes. Several granite war memorials honoring Riley County's dead dotted the perfectly-manicured courthouse lawn.

A waving flag identified the post office on the opposite side of the street. Other businesses on Main Street included a gas station, a Dollar-General store, a jewelry store, a bank, two restaurants, a pizza parlor, a funeral home, a hardware store, a car dealership, a law office, a medical clinic, a drug store, and a Hallmark store.

An ancient, red-brick elementary school with a large playground stood at one end of the street. The residential part of Main Street was on the opposite end of town from the school, causing children to walk past the businesses on their journeys to and from school.

The beautiful, spiraled Main Street Presbyterian Church graced one end of town, while the First Methodists congregated in a pristine, white-stone sanctuary on the opposite end of Pleasantville. Two large, rival grocery stores sat side by side on the outskirts of town, near the car wash and movie theater.

Although it was not a large town, by any means, it was adequate and allowed its residents to conduct most of their daily business within its narrow borders. Specialized business or hospitalization required a one-hour drive to the nearest city. Any product not found on Pleasantville's Main Street could easily be purchased at the city's attractive shopping mall.

The Stanniger sisters lived in one of the nicer homes on Main Street. A Victorian-style, white-frame home, it was probably one hundred years old with wide green shutters and delicate gingerbread trim. The wrap-around porch had been meticulously decorated with flowers in hanging baskets and ceramic pots. Hearty marigolds were still colorful and robust, seemingly thumbing their noses at the recent onset of chilly weather. Ears of Indian corn hung on a porch post, and a huge fall wreath adorned the heavy, oak door.

Parking my car directly in front of the house, I strolled leisurely up the sidewalk while clutching my notebook. In true girl-scout fashion, I was prepared for the meeting. I rang the bell and waited nervously. The lace curtains moved slightly and the door was unlocked.

Both ladies met me and cordially welcomed me into their home. The house smelled of lavender and spice. As we stood in the airy foyer under a crystal chandelier, I introduced myself: "My name is Margo Brown—I was Johnny's teacher."

The taller sister spoke first, "It's a pleasure to meet you, Mrs. Brown. I am Sadie Stanniger and this is my sister, Nora." Both smiled sweetly and showed no curiosity as to the purpose of my visit.

These pert ladies looked like old ladies ought to look,
I thought. They wore granny-glasses, and their wizened
faces were framed with silver curls. Both were wearing
dresses, and I wondered if they customarily wore them or
just hadn't changed their church attire. Nora wore a pink
cardigan sweater over her dress, while Sadie clutched a
white shawl around her narrow shoulders. One sister
wore a string of pearls, while the other spinster was em-
bellished by an ornate brooch fastened at her throat.
Their shoes were the black orthopedic type with laces;
they would definitely have been regarded as lethal in a
kicking contest.

Older people these days usually dress in jogging suits
and Reeboks and color their hair. Sometimes I have
caught myself wondering where all the old people have
gone. At funerals it's often hard to tell if the deceased is
coming or going. Although I respected the Stanniger sisters for their obvious acceptance of the "sunset years," I
seriously doubted if I would ever resign myself to blue
rinses or sensible shoes.

As they led me into the parlor, I was amazed at the ar-
ray of crocheted doilies on the backs and arms of
furniture . . . just like at sister Irene's house. Surely there
was some sort of genetic factor involved—maybe an un-
discovered crochet chromosome.

Childless women always love pets, and I was not surprised to see the yellow-striped tabby cat curled up
peacefully on a pillow near a heat register. Lacy, sheer curtains covered every window yet allowed much light to
filter into the room. Near the largest window stood a
birdcage, and upon closer examination I glimpsed a yellow canary perched on his tiny swing.

As I settled into a large, overstuffed chair, I revealed
the purpose of my visit: "You see, in addition to being a
teacher, I also do a little writing." They both smiled and
nodded with approval.

"During all my years of teaching, this is the first time that one of my students has been in a fatal accident. It made such an impact on my students and on the entire school, that I have decided to write a story about Johnny and his accident for an educational magazine. I need to know everything you can possibly tell me about Johnny, his family, and the circumstances surrounding his death." I spoke confidently as a woman of purpose and fervently hoped that lightning wasn't striking anywhere nearby.

My audience was clearly moved. They made soft, mewing noises of approval and became a bit misty-eyed. "How sweet of you," they almost said in unison.

With utmost sincerity I replied glibly, "It would be like a tribute to Johnny, and maybe teachers would read it to their classes; hopefully, other children wouldn't repeat Johnny's tragic mistake." Amazingly, I had almost convinced myself of my passionate mission.

Nora spoke, "If it saved only one child, it would be worth it." I agreed, and noticed what a tiny voice she had. I guess all those years of whispering in a library setting had modified her voice. She sounded exactly like a Walt Disney mouse. As she continued squeaking, I strived to remain focused.

So began our interview. Diligently, I took notes as the dear little ladies poured out their hearts.

"I want you to tell me everything you can remember about Johnny and his family," I said earnestly.

Sadie began, "Our dear sister Irene did all she could for her girls, but somehow. . .they just didn't turn out very well. She and Dale had a good marriage; he was a railroader and always had a secure job. They gave their girls a stable home, a fine Christian home."

I glanced around the room. A worn family Bible lay on the coffee table; several religious pictures hung on the walls. A beautiful, old upright piano sat nearby with hymnals propped open. These ladies were Baptists, and resoundingly so.

Nora picked up the story: "Francine. . .Franny, was always so smart, and they sent her to two different colleges. But she kept changing her course of study. First, she was going to be a nurse. Then, she decided to become a teacher. Later, she took up business classes and then quit college completely."

My mind wandered and I thought of how people who constantly change majors never end up with degrees, but they are certainly killers in Trivia Pursuit games.

At this juncture, sister Sadie joined in. "Now, Peggy was always rather slow. She could have been a big help at home to her parents, but she was always . . . " At this point, she widened her eyes, leaned forward, and whispered, "Boy-crazy." Her sister confirmed it with a nod. It was as if they had divulged some kind of a state secret.

"Tell me about Johnny's father," I said respectively.

"Well, no one knows for sure who he was; Peggy never would tell. She always insisted on privacy regarding the child's origins. But, she was hanging around with some construction workers who were traveling through town. Irene knew she was slipping out and seeing someone, but she couldn't stop her. Peggy was around twenty years old then. We all figured he was probably a married man," Nora stated, making no effort to hide her titanic disapproval.

Sadie chimed in, "It was almost time for the baby before anyone knew . . . she always was rather overweight, and she wore those loose tops." She paused. "She got testy and hateful and wanted to move out at the end . . . so they let her. They bought a trailer and fixed it up real nice for her and the baby. When Johnny was born, Irene went out there and helped her every day for a while, but then Peggy wanted to be alone. Irene and Dale checked in on her and the baby once a week after that; they took food and bought Johnny clothes and such. They did talk her into getting "fixed" so there wouldn't be any more babies; her labor had been hard, so she readily agreed to that."

"You know," Nora squeaked, "she was already receiving disability checks, and when the baby was born, she also started getting social security for him. I think it's called "Aid to Dependent Mothers." Dale had paid for the trailer, and her utilities weren't much; she had plenty of money."

"IF she had used it right," Sadie confided, pursing her lips as she paused. "She got to drinking and spending her money on alcohol. That's when the trouble started."

"What trouble?" I asked.

The sisters were most forthcoming in discussing the disgraceful episodes of their family's history. Nora said, "Well, she started neglecting Johnny; Irene and Dale threatened repeatedly to take him away from her. She'd do better for a while and then Irene would check; he'd be uncared for and the trailer would be filthy. Sometimes she was drunk, and Johnny was running around the trailer unattended with nothing to eat but crackers." She shuddered in disgust. "Irene took Johnny home, cleaned him up, and fed him many times. When Peggy sobered up, she begged and cried and repeatedly promised to stop drinking. They always trusted her and gave her so many chances to get Johnny back."

Sadie took a turn: "She got worse after Dale died; he developed cancer of the liver and went real fast . . . he only lived three months after they found it. Irene was so busy with Dale during that time that she didn't check on Peggy very often. Johnny's hair got so long people thought he was a little girl."

"And then one summer day, Peggy was out drinking and had left the boy home alone . . . he was probably four years old. She had actually tied him to the clothesline like a dog. He was just sitting there in the shade playing with his toys when his grandmother drove up. That was the final straw. She went to court and got custody of Johnny. Peggy was furious. She sold the trailer and moved away for a while, probably a year; but she finally came home and Irene let her move in with her. However, she made her help around the house and allowed no drinking. They got along tolerably well," Nora said.

"When Johnny went to kindergarten, the teachers said his language skills were extremely immature. His vocabulary was like a two-year old. Everyone thought he had a learning disability, but he didn't. Peggy just hadn't spent any time with him . . . you know, talking to him, reading to him, taking him places. She kept him in diapers for ever so long. His teachers found out real quick that he could learn; he had just been so deprived. They put headphones on him and had him to listen to tapes every day to increase his verbal skills. He always turned the volume up and the doctors declared that's why he talked so loudly . . . because he learned so many words from those tapes and said them along as he turned the pages of picture books," Nora continued.

"Those wonderful teachers worked with him; speech and hearing specialists spent hours with him. He caught up and went on to first grade right on schedule. They started him in a slow-reading class, but in no time at all, they had moved him to a regular group. He was a good little reader, and he made average grades all along," Sadie said proudly. "And Irene started taking him to church with her. He liked Sunday school and never missed a Sunday as long as his grandmother was alive. Of course, Peggy wouldn't go, and when Irene died Johnny didn't get to go anymore."

Nora stood and said almost royally, "I believe it's time for tea. Do you take sugar in yours, Mrs. Brown?"

"Yes, please . . . that would be very nice," I replied

thinking how appropriate it was for these quaint, little ladies to offer tea. I welcomed the sudden feeling that I was in a time warp, a time of slower days when ladies in dresses customarily served tea to Sunday-afternoon guests.

When Nora returned, she was carrying a lovely silver tray with a matching china teapot and cups. Square pieces of golden-brown spice cake had been arranged on saucers. The cake was delicious and I commented on the icing. Sadie offered, "It's mother's own recipe for burnt-sugar icing."

As I nibbled and sipped, I continued my investigation. "Franny and Peggy aren't very close, are they?"

"Oh, no," Sadie confided. "They don't have anything to do with each other. They had a big dispute when Dale and Irene made out their will."

"Why was that?"

"Well, Franny had a good husband. Hank was a trucker and he really loved Franny. He wanted children, but she wouldn't hear of it . . . said it would ruin her figure."

"That's too bad," I said simply, thinking how I've always hated being around women with exceptional figures. I have perpetually worn myself out trying to keep my stomach sucked in while in their presence.

"Yes, but he still loved her and provided well for her. But he was gone so much, on the road, you know." Sadie looked to Nora for support and received it in the form of a nod. "She got to running around on him . . . even with married men. Everyone knew. Finally, he filed for divorce and moved away. She broke that boy's heart!"

"Someone mentioned that Johnny was to inherit the farm," I began.

"Oh, yes," Nora replied quickly. "Dale and Irene were so aggravated with their girls; they knew they'd just sell the farm and run through the money. They had a lawyer make out the will, so Johnny would inherit the home and farm when he came of age. They said it was the only way to assure he'd be taken care of. And, if he wanted to go to college or start a business, he could use the farm money. It was to give him a start. They loved the little fellow and knew he'd need all the help he could get when they were gone."

"So who owns the farm now?"

Sadie looked thoughtful. "The will stated Johnny or his next-of-kin. They intended that to be his wife or children at his death. Of course, no one expects a child to die."

"It seems to me that his mother would be his next-of-kin now," I stated and winced at the implications.

Both ladies agreed that it certainly appeared so.

"How big is the Benson farm?"

"It's only one hundred and fifty acres, but it has high-grade coal under it; so that makes it extremely valuable. The coal company has mined right up the edge of the property. Dale was offered a good price for it several times, but he wouldn't sell it . . . wanted to save it for Johnny." Sadie looked down and wrung her handkerchief. "Poor baby," she whispered.

"What kind of care did Peggy give Johnny after her mother passed away?" Images of Johnny wearing ill-fitting clothes and needing a haircut came to mind.

Nora said, "Well, he was pretty much big enough by then to take care of himself. Sister and I drove out once in a while and took them food. Johnny loved our chicken and noodles, so we always made extra for them. Also, we always shared our vegetable soup; it is so nutritious. Peggy didn't cook much; they ate a lot of bologna sandwiches and potato chips. They drank soda pop with all their meals." She shuddered in disgust.

"Was she good to him?" I asked simply.

"We don't think she ever mistreated him—just neglected him, left him alone too much," Sadie said.

Suddenly I felt adventurous. "Who's Peggy's current boyfriend?" I asked boldly.

Both ladies widened their eyes and pursed their lips as they said almost in unison, "Oh dear, we wouldn't know about that."

Nora stated, "She never brought anyone around to meet us. Never once did she bring a man-friend to a family dinner."

"Johnny said something about his mother's friend," I offered. "Do you know of anyone who visited them?"

"Not really," Nora continued. "However, there is a man . . . the manager of the state forest. He lives alone in a trailer in the forest . . . not far from their house. Johnny talked about seeing him and talking to him on several occasions."

Sadie joined in, "Boyd Slattery. Irene did not like him and did not want Johnny around him. He had a beard and long hair, you know, like a hippie. She thought maybe he had been in jail at one time. We saw him once; he was a very strange man, unkempt and rude." I diligently wrote it all down.

She continued in a dismal voice. "We don't know what will happen to the girls now. Irene always tried to have everyone together for the holidays. Franny came and was always decent to Peggy at those times. Even Dale's nephew and his wife, Art and Junie Benson, joined us." She looked at her sister. "We thought we'd have the holiday dinners here this year. It certainly won't seem right without Irene or Johnny though," she said sadly. I offered an understanding nod.

"What do you know about the night of Johnny's death?" I asked in soft tones.

The sisters both shook their heads sadly. Sadie spoke: "Just what was in the paper. We never could bring ourselves to ask Peggy about the accident; it was just so sad for her. Making her talk about it seemed cruel and pointless."

After a respectful pause, I asked, "What do you think Peggy will do now?"

"She needs to do something," Nora stated. "Sister and I encouraged her to come to the senior citizens' center. She would enjoy the activities. We go on Monday for ceramics, Wednesdays for bingo, and Fridays for the outings. She could come along as a helper . . . it would be good for her." I agreed heartily and closed my notebook.

I stood and thanked the ladies for the refreshments and for their time. They walked me to the door and wished me luck in my writing. None of us had any idea how much luck I was going to need.

Franny's house sat on the outskirts of town. As I pulled up in front of the neat, little Cape Cod, I suddenly regretted not calling first. But for some obscure reason, I felt she would have made an excuse to not see me. So, I had decided to surprise Ms. Bumpus.

As I parked in her driveway and crossed her yard, I was not surprised to see two pink flamingos standing beside a crystal ball in the center of her lawn. I wondered if she would retire them to the garage for the winter or merely dress them for the season. I could only speculate on the outfits she might conjure up for them. If there were an Olympic event for putting together garish outfits, old Franny would bring home the gold.

She opened the door on the second ring and appeared as though I had disturbed a nap. "Hi, Franny," I began cheerfully, "I hope I'm not bothering you, but I was in the neighborhood and thought I'd stop."

She looked puzzled, but swung the door open and said, "No problem, come on in." As I followed her into the small living room, I scanned the area. Contemporary

furniture sat neatly between marble-topped tables. Collections of tiny glass figurines and silk flowers crowded the
surfaces. No doilies here, I thought.

On top of the television set was a "glamour-shot" of
Franny, made up like a movie star. Beside it was a picture
of Franny in a bikini swimsuit standing on a sand-swept
beach. I wondered if it was one of those thong suits that
had only a strip down the backside. It amazed me that after spending one's whole life trying to keep underwear
out of there, they'd go and invent a swimsuit designed
to be worn like that.

A large portrait of Elvis on black velvet centered the
main wall. The words, "The King" were emblazoned in
gold script across the bottom. Franny's domain was not
exactly an archive of the arts. I saw no books at all. An
I.U. football schedule lay on the coffee table beside several glamour magazines.

Franny was wearing a colorful caftan with a collection
of bold stars and stripes on it; it could have been a flag
for some underdeveloped country. Her nails were long
and shiny red; it was glaringly obvious that her stunning
nails were her top priority.

As we sat in matching striped chairs, I gave Franny my
"article about Johnny" story. She did not change her
expression, but offered me a can of diet cola. I declined.

"I can't tell you much about Johnny," she finally said.
"I hardly knew him. We were only together on holidays.
I did love him though, I guess. I felt real bad when he
died. He sure didn't have much of a life." She sipped her
diet drink thoughtfully. "With no father . . . and my sister for a mother, he didn't have a chance." Stoically, she
then gave me the same basic facts that her maiden aunts
had just shared with me.

"I had no idea you and Peggy were sisters, until I saw
you at the funeral home."

"We've never been close." Franny took a sip of diet cola

and then defended her position by stating, "She was always so whiney and lazy; Mom and Dad just babied her. There is no reason that she can't get a job and work like everyone else. I know she's not very bright, but she could still do something. She says it makes her nervous . . . big deal! Damn if my job doesn't make me nervous some days."

"I heard that Johnny was to inherit his grandparents' farm."

"Hell, yes! That's just typical. I got screwed out of my inheritance because Peggy had an illegitimate child." Her eyes narrowed with anger. "It was like they rewarded her for screwing up . . . bought her a trailer and everything. She couldn't take care of him; he should have been put up for adoption when he was born. But no, she ends up with the house, the car, and the whole damn farm!" I wondered if she would contest the will now that Johnny was dead.

"What about Boyd Slattery? Did Johnny spend much time with him?"

Franny wrinkled her nose in disapproval. "He's a screwball hippie . . . probably a druggie. I have no idea what Johnny did. Peggy wouldn't have cared if he did."

"Do you know who Peggy sees? She told me she might be getting married."

After allowing the news to soak in, Franny threw back her head and laughed loudly. "Who knows? She's been gonna get married a dozen times. She lives in a fantasy world."

"Do you think Peggy ever mistreated Johnny?"

"Naw, she just ignored him mostly. Why do you ask?" She looked puzzled by the question.

"I just wondered. I really need to go now," I said rather abruptly. As I stood to leave I inquired, "Do you have a picture of Johnny that I could borrow?"

She thought for a moment, then got up and said,

"Maybe, let me check." She headed for the kitchen and I followed at her heels.

Her kitchen looked as if it had never had a meal cooked in it. Several diet-cola cans and a Lean Cuisine carton were in the wastebasket; two drink glasses sat on a counter.

She rummaged through a drawer and came up with one of Johnny's school pictures. As I slipped it into the pocket of my jeans, I thanked her for it and for her time. She seemed anxious to see me out.

Driving away, I thought of how Franny's place looked like the home of a "kept" woman. I wondered who the man in her life was; surely there was one. Was the largesse of her lover supplementing her meager secretarial salary? Had someone stopped by for a drink on Saturday night? I had work to do.

At school on Monday morning, there was a hand-written note in my mailbox. It simply read: Please see me . . . and was signed by Dr. Fitzbaum. I stopped by his office on the way to my room. The good doctor was standing at the outer counter; he motioned me to come on back to his inner office. I followed him in and he closed the door.

My first thoughts were that he had reconsidered on the journal issue or just possibly that he was going to return it to me. But when I saw his ominous face, I knew I was profoundly in trouble. He was livid and made no attempt to hide his expression of enormous scorn.

When he spoke, he was so blatantly angry that his voice trembled: "Mrs. Brown, I thought I told you NOT to speak of this matter to anyone. You have been questioning everyone connected with Johnny Benson! What is the matter with you?"

Startled, I groped for words, "Dr. Fitzbaum, I meant

no harm. I didn't mention the possibility of foul play to anyone." I rattled on about my nonexistent article, but could tell he wasn't buying any of it.

He glared at me with a look that I had never seen him use. "I consider what you did as INSUBORDINATION! And I intend to write a formal reprimand and put it in your professional file. Do you understand what I am saying?"

I was so shocked that I could hardly answer. Appropriate words always come later. I mumbled a weak apology and felt angry tears sting my eyes. In stunned silence, I forced myself to be composed.

"Are you aware that you are being evaluated this year?" he asked with a threatening sneer. "I don't want to hear another word about this!"

Nodding, I moved numbly towards the door as the bell rang. At the last moment, I remembered and asked him if I could please have the journal. Through clenched teeth, he said, "I don't have it. I thought it was at home, but it wasn't; it must have been accidentally thrown away."

He was lying and I knew it; years in the classroom had given me much acumen in that area. As the door slammed behind me, I was hot to the soles of my feet. Walking to my room through throngs of noisy students, I was filled with two conflicting emotions: horror at the thought of having my virginal file violated and sheer elation that I had made copies of the journal pages.

Chapter Seven

For the rest of that day, I felt as if I were being held together by static electricity. So far, my unauthorized investigation had not gotten off to a very auspicious beginning.

When sixth period finally arrived, it was with impotent fury that I told Roxie about my brief, horrific visit to Dr. Fitzbaum's office. She listened intently and finally said, "Well, don't pop an artery—you tried."

"Tried? Don't you think for a minute that it's over!" I roared, my face flaming.

"Do you mean you are still going to pursue this?" she questioned. "Do the words 'job search' not mean anything to you?"

Hope lurked in the deep recesses of my mind that perhaps since Dr. F. had exploded and discharged all his overloaded circuits, he would forget the whole matter. It had undoubtedly been a power trip for him. By all rights, I should have felt intimidated and apprehensive, but I did not.

Rather, I felt exhilarated by the rightness of my quest. A grand and noble path lay before me—a path I felt compelled to journey upon. Johnny's enigmatic death hovered over me like a thick, gray cloud and demanded resolution.

"They can't fire me for asking questions;" I retorted with bravado, "I'm on tenure." Roxie and I had often mused over our evaluations. Our inspections every three years failed to create the panic they once had incited in us. Possessing confidence in our subject areas and classroom presentations—as only age and experience can bring, we rather enjoyed the audience. Maybe we were like two old racehorses who loved to trot around the track for visitors.

"We're in our final form now," we'd say proudly. "We can't improve any more—we're state-of-the-art!" We knew we had peaked professionally and wondered idly when the inevitable decline would hit that would mandate retirement.

Rather than join the affable group in the lounge, we sipped hot coffee at a table in the back of my classroom where we could confer in private. "I know who Fred is," Roxie stated. "Dottie Richter, my neighbor, drives the bus that Johnny rode. She said the only Fred on her bus is Fred Lankford."

"I don't recall a Fred Lankford coming through middle school," I replied. "He must have moved here later."

Roxie grinned conspiratorially, "Let's pull his file."

Within minutes, we were thumbing through index cards in the guidance office. Teachers had access to the student cards for parent names, addresses, and telephone numbers. As needed, we were encouraged to contact parents for conferences.

There was only one Lankford in our school file. Fred J. had moved to Riley County that fall and enrolled as a freshman. Almost sixteen years old, he had obviously been retained. His grades were deplorable. We noticed that he lived several miles from the Benson home. Making sure no one was watching, we copied down his class schedule.

At the moment, he was in a general math class with our least favorite colleague, Ms. Eleanor Eiscubus. A thirty-year veteran teacher, she was as hard as flint and emanated an icy chill whenever she passed through the hallways. She was blondish-gray, anorexic-thin, and kept her lips pulled tightly together in a perfect sphincter formation. Rarely seen to smile, she seemed to bear a grudge with the entire faculty with the exception of a chosen few. She was adamantly against everything and everyone.

When I first began teaching at JWR, I smiled and spoke in passing. She totally ignored any attempt of friendship or even co-worker recognition. Single and childless, she appeared to embrace a profound disgust for children. The kids referred to Ms. Eiscubus as, "Old Ice-Cube Ass." She was a nasty piece of work and always in a snit over something.

Roxie and I concluded that she was probably in the middle of a difficult menopause, which manifested itself by invoking acute irritability upon its victim. Whatever the cause, she had such an acid tongue we figured she could probably jump-start a car.

That very day, we had passed her stomping her way back from the cafeteria and had commented on her scowling countenance. "I wonder what she's so angry about today?" I asked quietly.

"Oh, she probably found too many F's in the vegetable soup," Roxie quipped. We chuckled and went our way, not knowing we would be visiting her classroom before the day was over.

I rapped politely on her classroom door and she answered immediately. It was one of the few times that she had ever made eye contact with me. "Hi," I said in my friendliest tone, "I'm sorry to disturb you, but could I speak to Fred for a moment?" I fully expected her to launch a verbal grenade and braced myself for the explosion.

Instead, she leveled a steely gaze at me, said nothing, and turned to her class. "Fred," was all she said. A gan-

gly, unkempt boy with long, disheveled hair rose slowly
to his feet and looked in our direction. I motioned for
him to come out into the hallway.

As he stepped into the hall, I closed the door quietly.
He slumped into a chair by the door undoubtedly placed
there for detention purposes. I pulled up a chair and sat
facing him. Roxie pretended to be reading announce-
ments on a nearby bulletin board.

"Yeah?" was his only response when I spoke to him.

"Fred, I know you rode the same bus as Johnny
Benson. He left a book in my room, and I wondered if
you could tell me where he lived, so I could return it." I
smiled.

"Who?" He asked in a surly tone. A real teacher hater.

"Johnny, you know, the boy who died. You have
been to his house, haven't you?"

"Oh, that little fat kid. Hey, I don't know where you
get that stuff. He rode my bus, but it ain't like we were
friends or nothing." His impudence and slouching demeanor made me want to smack him.

"I didn't say you were friends, I just thought you'd
been out there and could tell me where he lived."

"Naw, I don't know. He was already on the bus when
I got on in the mornings, and going home I got off before he did. I never saw his house." He kept his eyes
safely focused on the floor.

I moved right to the point. "Why were you mean to
him, Fred? He was a lot younger than you."

"Who said I was mean to him?" His dark eyes flashed
at me like a trapped wild animal.

"He told me. I just want you to tell me why you
picked on him." I stood to enhance my authority, a skill
I had acquired as a short teacher.

Suddenly his eyes narrowed with anger. "He was such
a little dork." He didn't even deny the allegation.

"And you're perfect." By then I was angry and determined that his indignation would not surpass mine. Glaring at him until he dropped his eyes and began picking at his dirty fingernails, I drew a deep breath and composed myself. My efforts to intimidate him were desperately lacking; I knew I'd never wreak a confession from him or cause him to betray his brotherhood.

I casually mentioned the lizard mania, and I could tell he had no idea Johnny usually had a lizard with him. He didn't seem bright enough to lie well. A classic bully, he was hateful and picked on young, vulnerable children because he had probably been mistreated. Patterns sometimes seem to be the only reliable entities.

"Can I go now?" he asked with a smirk. I dismissed him readily and turned to Roxie. She shrugged her shoulders and we retreated gratefully to our haven.

"What do you think?" I asked, candidly hoping she had picked up something I had missed.

"He's a loser, but I don't think he was lying," she replied. I agreed, but asked her to check out the bus situation with her friend Dottie.

Two days later, undeterred by Dr. F.'s admonitions and in pursuit of truth, Roxie and I were on our way to the state forest. The squat, concrete block building that housed the park office was near the entrance. Slattery's official vehicle, a jeep with "Riley State Forest" printed on the door, was the only vehicle in sight.

Parking next to it on the gravel lot, we approached the office door and noticed that it closed at five. We hadn't been able to leave school until three-thirty, and it had taken nearly twenty minutes to make the drive. Our plans were twofold: talk to Boyd Slattery at the office and check out his trailer while he was still at the office. We knew we didn't have much time.

When we entered the cluttered office, we found him smoking a cigarette—his boots propped up on his desk. A rangy, swarthy man, with long, dark hair and a full beard, he appeared more annoyed than startled at our unexpected visit. I began the conversation.

"Boyd Slattery?" I inquired innocently.

"Yep—what can I do for you?"

"Please allow us to introduce ourselves, Mr. Slattery. I am Margo Brown and this is Roxie Rayburn. We both teach at Riley Middle School." Not bothering to stand, he made no attempt to hide his scorn for educators.

"I hated school," he muttered with disdain.

Roxie spoke up, ignoring his insolent manner. "Mr. Slattery, we know you're a busy man, but we were wondering if you would consider speaking to our students sometime about the state forest." I noticed for the first time that she had worn pine trees on her ears for the occasion and her forest-green "Save a Tree" T-shirt.

He looked bewildered. "What? I ain't no speaker." Then he laughed a disgusting, guttural laugh. His tone was querulous and I didn't like him.

"Oh, you wouldn't have to be a great speaker. We hoped you could tell the kids about the wildlife, the trails. You know, you could bring in the environmental factors . . . like maybe on Earth Day." I could tell she was just making it up as she went.

With rough hands, he pushed some strands of greasy hair out of his eyes. I wondered if he really were a drug dealer like Franny had suggested. I'd always heard that druggies lose the will to groom. Although he was probably only a little schizoid, he was very intimidating. He was dressed in camouflage jacket and pants as though prepared for an air attack.

Except for a pitted complexion, he wasn't a bad-looking man; there was a rather rugged handsomeness about him. It was difficult to ascertain his age; he could have been anywhere between thirty-five and forty-five years old. His long legs shifted suddenly and he stood abruptly. "Nope—not interested, Ladies. Now if you'll excuse me, I need to close up . . . gotta shut the gates and check some feeding stations before five."

I jumped in. "Mr. Slattery . . . Boyd, are there many poisonous snakes in the forest?"

He stared coldly at me as if I had struck a nerve. "Not many, but I see one now and then."

"What kind?"

The taciturn Slattery took a deep breath and exhaled slowly as if in deep thought. "There's copperheads along the creeks, and once in a while I see a rattler."

"Sure was too bad about the Benson boy," I interjected.

He nodded and began closing drawers and rolling maps in preparation to leave. "Did Johnny ever talk to you about snakes?" I asked.

His hands stopped and he leveled mud-brown eyes at me. "Naw, he was always hunting lizards." His words were cold and stinging.

"Did he come here very often?"

"Just a couple times on his bike; it was pretty damn far for him to ride."

"Did he visit you at your trailer very often?"

He paused as if in deep thought and then said, "It ain't too far from his house. He played in the forest a lot, and sometimes he wandered over my way."

"Did you spend much time with him?"

He stared at me briefly and then said without remorse, "Hell, no, I used to run him off. Don't like kids hanging around pestering me. If I wanted kids, I'd have got married and had my own." His tone was truculent and his breath charged with cigarette smoke.

"He was a lonely boy," I said. "I just wondered if any-body ever warned him about poisonous snakes."

"Not me, now I need to go." He spoke abruptly.

"Of course, thank you for your time. If you change your mind about speaking to our classes, just let us know."

He stared at us ferally. "Don't hold your breath," was all he said as we left.

We parked the car just around the bend from the Benson house, so Peggy wouldn't see it and began walk-ing through the forest towards Boyd Slattery's trailer site. Following the electric lines from the road we tried to imagine how Johnny would have walked. Evening was arriving earlier and earlier as October waned, and we knew darkness would claim the forest prematurely.

We crossed a winding creek via a fallen log and followed a path up a small hill. After cresting the top we came upon a narrow dirt road that wove its way through tall trees and past tangles of brushy weeds. Dry leaves rustled beneath our feet.

After ten minutes of hiking, the road turned and fol-lowed a rocky bluff towards the river. Grateful that we had changed into tennis shoes after school, we moved as quickly as possible through Johnny's turf. Suddenly, a brown and beige trailer with a dented front awning loomed through the trees.

Standing behind a clump of persimmon trees we sur-veyed the area. The shabby trailer and overgrown yard affirmed our suspicions that Boyd Slattery might have had a glorious career as a mountain man. The area resembled a hunting or fishing camp with outdoor tables for clean-ing wild game or fish. Steel traps dangled haphazardly from a tree and several bait buckets were overturned. A sagging clothesline ran across the front yard with some kind of a fishing net draped over it. Several metal oil

drums stood along one end of the trailer, and an assortment of discarded tires and junk cluttered the entire
scene. An ancient and dented pick-up truck with multi-
colored doors was parked near the trailer home.

Stealthily we approached the truck and peeked
through the cracked windows. It looked like a portable
dumpster. Rags, old boots, newspapers, and beer cans littered the seat and floor.

Suddenly, ear-splitting barks and yelps began erupt-
ing from an unseen and unfriendly, but apparently
nearby dog. In true panic, Roxie and I tacitly and simultaneously agreed to hastily clamber into the back of the
truck. At that point, our case lost most of its whimsical
charm. Trembling and hugging each other we scanned
the area, but could not locate the source of the horrify-
ing din. When our adrenaline levels had returned to
normal, we noticed that the threatening sounds did not
get any closer.

After a few minutes of cautious search, armed with large
sticks, we located the source of the dangerous sounds. A
chain-link enclosure behind the trailer housed a fierce and
lethal-looking pit bull. It always seemed strange to me
that people who appear to have nothing always need huge
dogs to protect it. I couldn't imagine what anyone could
steal from that place.

Keeping out of the dog's viewing range, we bolstered
up enough courage to slink to the trailer and peek into
an uncurtained window. The trailer was as messy as the
truck, only on a grander scale. It looked as if a small war
had been fought in it.

It was a good thing that Boyd Slattery had chosen not
to marry; a woman would have killed the slob. The trash
flow was at flood stage as beer cans and empty pizza car-
tons had piled up in the wastebasket, cascaded over the
sides, and mounded against the wall. Clothes were strewn
everywhere, and some kind of a motor sat among tools

on the kitchen table. Girly posters decorated the paneled walls and a Playboy calendar hung by the phone.

"What do you think?" Roxie asked as I jumped down from the trash can that had been my peeping post.

"I'm glad he ran Johnny off. He sure didn't need to be hanging around this guy," I said decidedly.

Roxie bent over and picked something out of the grass. "Well, look what I found," she said simply, "a joint."

She carefully handed me the twisted remains of a marijuana joint. Roxie's science classes studied various types of drugs and their effects, and maybe her past included some first-hand experience for all I knew, but I was naive. I would never have noticed the joint and wouldn't know a marijuana plant if one came up and bit me.

"Maybe he IS a drug dealer," I said, "which would explain his profound distaste for visitors. What should we do?"

"One joint doesn't mean he is a dealer. Let's check out his trash," she stated emphatically.

It sounded good, but neither of us had thought to bring a flashlight, and we knew he'd notice if we took his whole trash can. We lifted the lid, but the stench drove us back, and we decided it was not worth the effort. I wasn't sure what we were looking for anyway.

As we drove away, we enjoyed an excessive spurt of high spirits and decided that Boyd Slattery was definitely a prime suspect. Maybe there WAS something valuable enough at his home to merit a fierce watchdog. If he were a drug dealer, he would have reason to not want Johnny around. And if Johnny knew something, he would have had a motive to kill him.

I recalled the lines from Johnny's journal: "I have a secret, I have a mouth . . . " It certainly would have been easy for him to put a poisonous snake in Johnny's lizard box. Was he the mystery man who was courting Peggy

Benson? Did he plan to marry Peggy and enjoy Johnny's inheritance? My hopes were borne high on the updraft of that newest revelation, and I felt assurance slip solidly back into place. It was time to go to the sheriff.

After school on Friday, I went to see Burley Haggard alone. Roxie was not in any trouble with Dr. Fitzbaum, and I wanted to keep it that way. She was interested in the case but it was passion to me. Although I knew I was bordering perilously on insubordination and my methods were unorthodox, I felt a deep need to complete my odyssey.

Deputy Sonny Ray met me in the outer office, thumbs cocked into his belt loops. "Evening, Miss Brown, what can I do for you?"

"I need to speak to the sheriff."

"Got some young'un you want him to arrest?" He laughed coarsely. "Well, Ma'am, he's in a meeting. Can I help you?"

"No, thank you, Sonny Ray—I really need to speak to Burley. I don't mind waiting." I settled into a wooden chair.

"Suit yourself," he said and smiled genially. He could be a nice guy when he wasn't making an ass of himself.

Time did not hang heavy on me, as I had some papers that needed grading in my canvas tote bag. After about ten minutes, a plump, balding man came out. He exchanged a few clandestine words with Sonny Ray, at which they both roared with laughter, and then he left.

Discomfited, I poised on the edge of my chair and waited for permission to enter Burley's office. As time passed my heart hammered, and I could feel the pulse pounding in my ears. There was no going back.

After what seemed to be light years, Burley appeared and cordially invited me into his office. "And what can I do for you, Mrs. Brown?" he asked sunnily as he motioned me to a seat.

Burley, a square, paunchy man with a thick, gray shock of hair was probably more than sixty years old. He had a baby-butt face, soft and pink with full cheeks and few lines. His only blemish was a large, round brown mole on his right cheek bone. From my angle it vaguely resembled an undeveloped third eye; my mind wandered momentarily to aliens.

Although Sheriff Haggard was known as an honest man and of good reputation, he was also a "red-neck." And that part of him couldn't be changed any more than his blood type. It was likely that he was a closet Klansman, and that was presumably acceptable with the majority of his constituency. Since there were no minorities in Riley County, his prejudice was legend and solely expressed in talk from afar.

A few years ago he told me of his older brother's marriage. "I don't blame Wallace," he said. "I'd get married again myself if anything happened to Mama. Couldn't abide living alone. In fact, if there was no one left on Earth but me and a black man, I'd say: 'Move over, brother, I'm a-movin' in.'" He told the story with relish as if it were honorable and a credit to his good name. I was appalled at his bigotry.

As I poured my stirring story out to Burley, he drummed his fingers on his glass-topped desk and listened intently. Covering all bases, I relayed the conversations with Peggy Benson, the aunts, and Boyd Slattery. From memory I recounted everything that had been in Johnny's journal and my insights of foul play. Launched like a rocket, I even covered all the details of my reprimand.

He nodded and appeared to consider each facet of the story. Only when I asked him not to tell Dr. Fitzbaum of our meeting did he show consternation. He gazed at me as if I had just desecrated the flag.

"Not tell the school principal?" he asked in his gravel-like voice. "That doesn't seem like good politics."

"Please Burley, let's just keep this between us. He means well, but I just think he's wrong. All I'm asking is that you reconsider the evidence and motive. It just seems that someone should check out this Boyd Slattery; maybe he has a criminal record. I know you can run checks on suspicious people."

He looked thoughtful and then asked, "Do you have the boy's journal with you?"

"That's another point. The journal has disappeared; I gave it to Dr. Fitzbaum two weeks ago. It seems to have been misplaced or accidentally thrown away."

"That's too bad. It could be needed evidence."

"I thought maybe he had shown it to you."

He shifted uneasily, "No, I haven't talked to Dr. Fitzbaum since school started."

Almost without thinking, I spouted, "But I thought you were at school . . . in his office, right after I left it with him." I was sure Roxie had told me she had seen him there.

"No, Ma'am. I wish otherwise. It's sure too bad that journal's gone." He spoke with defeated finality. "Like I said, it could have been important evidence."

I brightened, "But I made copies . . . I still have my copies."

His face changed, and I did not quite understand what was happening. He paled, stared at me briefly, and then smiled slowly. "Do you have them with you?" he asked, his face alight with curiosity.

"No," I lied and I was not sure why. It was one of those built-in, woman things. "They're at school," I offered, "but I told you everything they contained. I have read them so often; I almost have them memorized."

Standing up, he said amiably, "All right, Margo, I'll do

some checking on Slattery. I'll also check with the court records about Johnny's inheritance. If there was anything amiss, we'll find it. Don't worry yourself over it. You did the right thing."

"And our little secret?"

"And it will be our little secret," he said, standing and shaking my hand.

The weekend was cool but crisp and beautiful with skies the color of robins' eggs. Friends who own a pontoon boat invited Dew and me along with two other couples for an all-day excursion on Saturday. We purchased buckets of fried chicken from a local convenience store and loaded coolers filled with cold drinks, salads, and fruit into our trunks. My plate of freshly-baked brownies scented our car as we drove the forty-five minute drive to Pike Reservoir, an eight-thousand acre lake built ten years ago solely for recreational purposes.

Stressed by my week's encounters, the respite was most welcome. As we leisurely spent the day on the placid and shimmering lake fishing, playing cards, talking and laughing; I basked in the golden sunshine and reveled in the warmth and security of friendship.

Bonded together by years of child rearing, we had cheered each others' kids on at various school activities and 4-H fairs. Graduation and birthday parties had been joint affairs. Fourth of July barbecues and New Year's Eve parties had become a tradition among our families. We had even taken several summer vacations together. Since our wedding dates were in close proximity, we four couples planned to celebrate our thirtieth anniversaries together with a long-awaited trip to Hawaii.

Although we engaged in lengthy discourse over many topics on that bronze October day, I did not share my unfolding Johnny drama. It had temporarily been put to rest; I had turned it over to Sheriff Burley Haggard and trusted that he would take care of it. Introspection brimmed with satisfaction, and my lofty principles assured me that I had done the right thing; truth and justice would prevail.

Sunday passed uneventfully. After church, Dew made his famous mushroom-cheese omelets for brunch, and we spent the afternoon raking and winterizing the yard and storing our deck furniture in the barn. The inevitable first freeze was imminent. We walked Sasha and made our customary Sunday-evening telephone calls to our college kids. All was well; it was a near-perfect weekend.

When I entered my classroom on Monday morning, icy shivers tip-toed up my spine. I knew immediately that someone had been in my desk and into my computer files. Although nothing was missing, I knew instantly what had been the subject of the search. As I stared in disbelief, I clutched my canvas tote bag close to my chest and whispered a thankful prayer that I had put nothing pertaining to the case on computer disks, and that I had kept my notes and the only copies of the journal pages with me all weekend.

Chapter Eight

Claude Dupree, ruthless assistant principal, was in my room within minutes of my reporting the rifling of my desk and computer.

"What was taken?" His tone was militant as usual.

"Nothing."

"Nothing? How do you know anyone was here?"

"Believe me, I know. Everything has been moved and shifted around. Look, I always keep my stapler right here, and now it is there." I pointed to prove my case. "And my gradebook and planbook have been moved, and my colored markers were never turned that way!" He stared at me as if I were insane.

"Margo, was there anything valuable in your desk?"

"Well, here's my solar calculator and some video tapes . . . " I said as I pointed to each item. "Oh, yes, here is an envelope with money collected for TAB paperback books." At that, I dumped the folder of money onto the desktop and counted out seventeen dollars and thirty-five cents. When I collected money from students to order bookclub books, I didn't usually leave it at school, but this time I had.

"Is it all there?" he asked as he leaned over my desk.

"Yes, it's all there," I said as I indicated the amount penciled on the envelope.

"Well," he said in a tone of relief, "since nothing was taken, I would assume that it was probably a student looking for answers to a test. No great harm done, I would say."

"I'm not giving any tests right now," I protested. "My students are involved in writing projects and poetry. There would have been no need to look for test answers. And what about my computer? Someone has tipped the screen of my monitor and moved my disk file; the disks are even out of order!" I had no intention of allowing him to invalidate my case.

Claude was wearing a navy blazer over a crisp, white-collared, pin-striped shirt. His tie was silky with muted tones of scarlet and mauve, while gray flannel slacks draped expensively over his glossy loafers. He strolled around my classroom, eyes wandering as he spoke: "These rooms are unlocked for cleaning during the evening hours. Sometimes kids who stay after school for extracurricular activities wander around the building."

He turned and looked at me briefly. "Of course we discourage that, but you can't watch all of them all the time. There was football practice last night, band over the weekend, and rehearsal for the fall drama production. Also, there was a cross-country meet here; people come into the building to use the restrooms. Chances are someone was just fooling around with the computer; some kids love to do that. If nothing was taken or damaged, I would say that you were lucky."

After he had circled the room, he returned to my desk and met my eyes. "I'll issue a memo tomorrow to remind all the teachers to keep a closer eye on their after-hours students." Claude spoke casually and with finality.

I couldn't tell him what I knew was being sought. I dismissed the issue with a conciliatory nod and vowed to be ever-vigilant. At my next free period I made extra copies of the journal, so Roxie and I would each have a set.

As soon as school was dismissed on Tuesday, Roxie and I headed for Indianapolis. We had dutifully volunteered earlier to attend a workshop designed to aid teachers in dealing with gifted and talented students. Various professional workshops were offered during the course of the school year, and it was highly encouraged for teachers to occasionally attend one. Some were beneficial and some were a total waste of time; one never knew until one went.

Roxie and I hadn't been to a workshop since we had attended a computer-awareness seminar a couple of years before. We thought this one would be a welcome and refreshing change of pace. All expenses were paid by the school corporation: meals, gas, and an overnight stay at a nice hotel. A substitute teacher was procured to teach our classes on Wednesday, while we were enlightened by the newest developments in pedagogy. It was one of the perks of our noble profession.

The three-hour drive to the city gave us ample time to discuss the case. As I drove and munched an apple Roxie began: "My neighbor, Dottie . . . the bus driver, confirmed what Fred Lankford said. He truly was on and off the bus after and before Johnny. Johnny had one of the longest rides of any of the kids since he lived out so far. She said she had never noticed Fred bothering Johnny, but admitted that she couldn't watch the kids all the time and still drive. However, she didn't think it could have amounted to too much, or someone would have told her." We agreed that Fred still could have slipped over to Johnny's house and planted the rattlesnake, but it seemed unlikely.

Roxie had also talked with Art Benson, Peggy's cousin. "Art told me that his Uncle Dale had been offered half a million dollars by the coal company for the farm, but he wouldn't sell . . . wanted to hold on to it for Johnny's future."

"Wow . . . that's quite an inheritance! Enough for someone to kill for, no doubt."

"When I asked Art Benson who owned the farm now, he said he figured it would be Peggy, since she was technically Johnny's 'next-of-kin.'"

"Did he seem like a decent fellow?" Now I was suspecting everyone, since the amount was so tempting.

"A real decent fellow. He's a mechanic over at Fairmont and his wife is a nurse. They have a four-year old son named Hershel. They are religious . . . almost to the point of being zealots." She paused. "It's not an old family farm; he would have no rights to it anyway. Dale and Irene Benson bought it after their marriage, probably for a song. He worked for forty years on the railroad and always made a decent income."

"Surely Franny will contest the will," I offered.

"She may, but I haven't heard anything."

"Had Johnny lived, she would have gotten nothing— but with him dead, she'll probably end up with half the farm." We wondered how badly Franny wanted that inheritance . . . enough to kill for? There was definitely motive.

As we traveled, we reflected on the different characters involved and recalled all the dialogue with them. All arrows pointed to Boyd Slattery. We had hopes that Burley would come up with something on him.

"Why do you suppose they keep such a creep as Boyd Slattery on as the park manager?" I asked.

Roxie was thoughtful. "Well, it's not too much of a job, as jobs go. Probably doesn't pay twenty thousand a year. And who'd want to have to live out there?"

"Only someone like Slattery, a loner, a woods-hermit," I replied. I wondered if he grew dope in the forest and stashed it in remote areas . . . something else to check out.

"From the looks of him and his place, it doesn't take much money to support his life style," Roxie said. "He probably buys his clothes at the same store as his hardware."

I reiterated my conversation with Sheriff Burley Haggard and that he denied speaking to Dr. Fitzbaum since school had started. Roxie was livid. "He's lying! I'm sure I saw him going into Dr. F.'s office on the Monday after you gave him Johnny's journal. I remember thinking they were probably discussing if it were relevant or not." Roxie was adamant. "It was the same day that Leo told you that it was nothing."

"Why would Burley lie about it?" I pondered aloud. "Maybe Dr. Fitzbaum had asked him not to mention their visit. But why?"

"Maybe they discussed it, decided it was nothing, and just wanted you to forget about it. So they let on as if it were so unimportant that it didn't even merit discussion." Roxie was probably right, but something kept gnawing at me.

When we arrived in Indy, I wondered idly why anyone would choose to live in a big city. As small-town and country people we invariably felt like aliens approaching a new planet when we entered a bustling city. The noise, the traffic, and the proliferation of buildings and people always overwhelmed our senses.

We checked into the plush, downtown Mariott Hotel, an ornate and comfortable oasis for us. Each of us had an overnight bag, and I had my tote bag containing the copied journal pages and stack of detailed notes pertaining to the case. My vigilance would not have increased had I been carrying around the Rosetta Stone.

Since our meals were to be reimbursed, we feasted that evening on Maine lobster and asparagus salad in the posh hotel restaurant. After a leisurely meal, we mingled in the lobby with other educators from all over our fine state and browsed through the selected literature piled upon long exhibit tables. I always enjoyed meeting teachers from other corporations; they hadn't seen my two dresses.

Our insipid name tags read: "Hello . . . my name is . . ." Roxie wanted to write "Donald Duck" on hers, but I discouraged it. Most of our colleagues had scrawled signatures that defied being read by the human eye, but we could always read the perfect stick and circle names of the elementary teachers.

After perusing the proffered pamphlets and accumulating some freebie pins, note pads, and magnets, we headed for our room. Some of our colleagues would remain in the spacious lobby and later in the smoky, dimly-lit bar until it closed exchanging lofty ideas and revelations, but not the Riley County delegates. Although keeping abreast of current educational trends and enlightenments was important to us, we planned to compact that part of our stay into a neat time block leaving us opportunity for some rest and relaxation on the side. We needed a change of pace, and basically we hoped the venture would just be a real hoot.

After showering and donning pajamas, we propped pillows against the headboards of our beds and made ourselves comfortable for our evening's entertainment. We had picked "Fried Green Tomatoes" from the rental-movie selection in the lobby. As we laughed and cried and admired the avenging "Towanda," we decided to throw discretion to the wind and call room service. We had magnanimously decided that it was time for dessert.

Within a few minutes, two huge, hot-fudge sundaes topped with whipped cream, nuts, and cherries were delivered to our door. Although we knew we'd probably have technicolor nightmares, we decided it was worth it. And we justified the calories by declaring that we had already lost control of our bodies; gravity was definitely winning, so it really didn't matter.

"Isn't this the life of Riley?" Roxie asked as she scooped through the whipped cream.

"We must pace ourselves," I replied languidly. "We still have tomorrow." I had no idea then how big tomorrow was to be.

Morning arrived too soon, and still full of lobster and ice cream, we hastily grabbed coffee and granola bars from the sumptuous breakfast buffet and made our way to meeting room number seven for our eight o'clock seminar.

Nearly two hundred educators gathered around long tables set up for Dr. Yon Yoko's workshop on "Dealing with Gifted and Talented Students in the Classroom." The tables were covered with white linens, and each boasted a water pitcher and a stack of disposable cups.

As most educators, we truly did want to learn new and better ways to deal with those exceptionally bright children, who constantly need to be challenged. As the morning progressed, we collectively hoped the event would be productive, but the best way to describe it was that it was unbelievably boring.

Dr. Yoko, whose build resembled that of a fire hydrant, appeared to be reading to us from a textbook . . . evidently one he had written. His voice was painfully monotone, as he rambled on and on interminably about theories of educational development. If he made eye contact, we couldn't tell due to his thick glasses.

As he droned on and on about higher-level thinking skills, it became increasingly obvious to us that Dr. Yoko was truly gifted. Though disheartened, Roxie and I were astute enough to realize that he had put together a workshop and gone from state to state suckering school systems into sending teachers to it—under the pretense that they might actually gain valuable insights and teaching techniques for teaching gifted and talented students. Each teacher present had been funded by his or her school corporation to the tune of a hefty one hundred and fifty dollar enrollment fee.

We educators had traveled to Indianapolis in search of intelligent life, and although the workshop was certainly not the world-class adventure we had hoped for, we sat like amiable toads in harmony of purpose. I thought about the story of the emperor and his new clothes and wanted to stand up and scream, "THIS IS A BIG WASTE OF TIME!" But I did not. However, from the jaded expressions and glazed eyes of my nearly—comatose colleagues, I realized that the attitude was profoundly pervasive. There was no discord in our ranks; we were bored in unison.

As we sat from eight until eleven o'clock, time passed with glacier speed. Roxie and I wanted desperately to jump ship and find a mall, but professional integrity disallowed it. When we broke for lunch I was amazed by the passivity of our colleagues. Most of the teachers were blithe about it, as if conditioned by years of sheer and unrelenting boredom in the name of education. But I was outraged at the waste of money and my time, which was growing more valuable to me each year. How the zealous guardians of the public purse could condone financing such a profoundly banal ruse was beyond my comprehension. It should have been a source of incredible shame to every tax-paying American.

The afternoon session, which ran from twelve until three, was even worse than the morning segment. It was such a yawn; we felt like felons serving time. I wanted to rush to the podium, grab the little man, and push his fast/forward button. We fought an irresistible urge for flight. The shopping mall called to us loudly.

Sometimes an overload of tension and boredom stimulates my entertainment gland, and I entertained Roxie with doodles and zany captions on my notepad. We ardently longed for a deck of cards and would probably have killed for a mini T.V. with headphones. By way of notes we concluded that Dr. Yoko was probably not even a true Japanese, that he had most likely just had his eyes fixed to lend credibility, and chances were that he couldn't even use chopsticks.

Finally, the session ended and we were set free. Emancipated, bleary-eyed educators bolted like rats. As we loaded our gear into the car and prepared to leave, Roxie said wearily, "Well, that concludes whatever in the hell happened here!"

Since rush-hour traffic is like a war in progress, we decided not to shop as planned but to head for home. Exhausted with the fatigue that comes from hours of idleness, we did not want to deal with the afternoon cattle drive from the city. We left Indy at three-thirty and expected to be home at six-thirty. I called Dew and informed him of our impending departure; he promised to have a pot of hot chili soup ready . . . succor for the returning warrior.

I have always been a cautious driver and have been known to boast that I have never had a ticket or a wreck. Admittedly, I am what's known as a "Sunday-afternoon driver." I rarely pass anyone and always drive just below the speed limit. It drives my kids crazy, and they frequently make such remarks as: "Watch out, Mom, a glacier is getting ready to pass us!" and "Gee, I hope the seasons don't change before we get there!" When they accuse me of driving at trolling speed, I remind them of my impeccable driving record.

Just out of the city, I attempted to brake for merging traffic when I realized that my brakes weren't braking properly. I pumped them as hard as I could, but for some inexplicable reason they were absolutely gone. Incredulity gave way to fear as I realized that we were gaining momentum coming down a hill, and I would soon over-run the traffic in front of me. "OH, NO!" I yelled, "My brakes are gone!"

Aghast, I swung into the passing lane but could see that I was gaining too fast in that lane too; so I zagged from lane to lane between cars, passed the car on my right, and finally drove off the road onto the grassy shoulder. As I saw a road sign approaching, I swerved down an embankment in frantic desperation. In the next flashing moments we hurtled down the embankment bumping along, dodging utility poles and trees.

Even with seat belts and shoulder straps intact, we bounced like popcorn in a popper. I felt like we were on a runaway bobsled to Hell and thought of my family as I tried not to smash into the whirling scenery. If there had been a black box, there would have been no calm, brave "May Day" proclamation as valiant pilots leave behind as they face inevitable death. Rather, I remember making high, nasal shrieks all on one note and more like a wounded animal than a human, as we catapulted along towards some kind of rambling industrial building. So occupied with my own hysteria, I had forgotten Roxie until she screamed, "HOLY SHIT!" as we leveled out, shot through several dumpsters, scraped against two trees, and finally came to a scrunching, jerking halt.

We sat in stunned silence and trembled for a few quiet seconds amidst a smell of steam and hot metal. With shaking hands, we undid our seat belts and looked around us. The front of the car was in a drainage ditch and only a few yards from an apparently abandoned factory building; it could have been worse. The passenger door was on the heavily damaged side and would not open, so we both crawled out on my side to survey the damage.

There was hardly a hand-span on the passenger side of the car that was not scraped or dented. Steam was hissing from the radiator and the muffler was lying in the grass some twenty yards up the embankment. One headlight was dangling from its casing. Nerves a'shamble, we agreed that the car looked like it was ready to be booked for a demolition derby.

A deep voice called from the roadside: "You ladies okay?" A semi truck was parked off the side of the road and the trucker stood looking down at us . . . ladies in distress.

Still spinning and queasy, I called out affirmation in an unsteady voice. "We're okay."

The tall, thickset young man lumbered down the sloping distance and approached us. "Whoa!" he said and whistled through his teeth, "You sure tore the hell out of your car. What happened?" He took off his cap and ran freckled fingers through his sandy hair.

"My brakes went out . . . I don't know what happened," I gulped. "They just weren't there!" I was still trying to reason it out. Nothing like this had ever happened to our cars before. Dew always kept our vehicles in tip-top condition. "Could you give us a ride to a gas station so we can use a phone?" I tried to not sound like a first-class wimp, even though my voice was quavery.

"I'd be happy to, ladies, but it looks like we have company," he replied glancing up the embankment.

A state police car had stopped on the shoulder of the highway. We waved good-bye to the gracious trucker and waited for the trooper to approach. He was a nondescript, middle-aged man with glasses and a stoic manner. Mainly he was concerned if we had been run off the road, or if we had been drinking. Since both answers were negative, and my license and registration were acceptable, he seemed ready to move on to bigger fish. If he had insisted on a breath test, Roxie and I, who both would have probably registered a 9.9 on a 1-10 level stress test at that moment, would have most likely attacked him. And considering our collective frame of mind . . . we could have taken him, I'm quite sure.

He gave us a ride to a modern Shell service station and reminded me to fill out accident forms with my insurance company within five days. We thanked him and found a telephone. I called Dew and interrupted the chili process. He called for a tow truck and then headed for Indianapolis in his red truck to rescue us. Roxie called Denzil and left a message on his answering machine; artists never answer telephones.

After three hours of walking the greasy floor of the gas station and drinking black coffee, we were so wired it was a wonder our hair wasn't standing up like porcupine quills when Dew finally arrived with our reprieve. After checking the battered car over, Dew declared that its frame was most likely sprung and that it was time to start car-shopping. Since that's one of his favorite pastimes, I was surprised that we didn't stop on the way home and road test some zippy, little number.

But we didn't. The ride home was three more hours, and no one had much to say. We were desolate and shaken. All I wanted was to get home to a hot shower and my bed. However, I did end up eating some midnight chili and it was good.

Neighbors who run a used-car lot and body shop had gone after the car that evening and towed it to their shop. They had promised to check it over and try to ascertain what had caused the brakes to malfunction.

They called the next morning at seven-thirty and Dew answered the phone. As he listened, his face grew ashen. As he gently replaced the phone in its cradle, he faced me and said: "They found out why your brakes didn't work."

"Why?" I asked anxiously.

"The brake lines had been very neatly cut."

Puzzled, I countered, "What does that mean?"

Dew's face was more serious than I had ever seen it, and his words cut into me like a sudden and icy blast of wind as he said: "It means that someone tried to kill you, Margo."

Chapter Nine

After meeting in my classroom for reconnaissance on Friday morning, Roxie and I resolutely stomped off for Dr. Fitzbaum's office. Someone had some questions to answer, and we couldn't think of a better place to start.

Franny motioned for us to go on back, and we were soon standing in front of our principal's wide, oak desk. Sipping coffee, he looked up peacefully and smiled as he set his cup down.

"Who knew we were at the Mariott in Indianapolis for the gifted and talented workshop?" I asked, getting right to the point. I was in a no-nonsense mood.

He pursed his lips as if in thought and then answered calmly, "Well, since it had been arranged for a good while, I imagine quite a lot of people knew about it. Why do you ask?"

"We want names, Dr. Fitzbaum," Roxie implored as she whipped out a small notepad and twirled a ballpoint pen to engage it into writing position.

He looked a bit troubled, but scratched his chin and spoke slowly: "Of course, all the office staff knew where you were. And I believe it was mentioned to your substitute teachers when they were called . . . Franny would have to tell you for certain about that." He paused for a moment as if in deep thought. Then he said rather matter-of-factly, "Presumably, other people in your depart-ments who had the option of going to the workshop knew where you were."

"Did anyone call here for us and ask where we were?" I was grasping at straws.

He leveled his gaze at me. "Not to my knowledge. Now are you going to tell me what this is all about?"

"Someone sabotaged our car while it was parked at the Mariott." I leaned on his desk and stared into his gray eyes. "The brake lines were cut; we could have been killed!"

Dr. Fitzbaum's eyes widened. "Are you certain they were cut?" His voice was almost a whisper.

"Absolutely. And it had to have been done by someone who knew of our whereabouts. That's why it's crucial that we know who knew of our location."

"Why would anyone want to harm you or Roxie?" His expression was one of absolute bewilderment.

I stood up straight and looked squarely into his eyes. "Because of what we know about Johnny Benson."

His interest perked at those words. "Mrs. Brown, you aren't still pursuing that idea, are you? I thought we had decided the issue was dead." His words were sharp and succinct.

I gave every indication that I had faithfully obeyed his injunctions. After all, it WAS my evaluation year.

He seemed to relax. "You ladies must realize that cities are dangerous places. Crimes are committed every day against innocent people."

"We are aware of that," Roxie stated stolidly.

Dr. Fitzbaum took a deep breath and exhaled slowly. "Let's not let our imaginations run riot here. Chances are, some street punks picked your car at random and vandalized it just for kicks. They had no idea who you were; you were just parked in the wrong place at the wrong time. It happens all the time; some kids get their jollies from causing trouble." His voice became much gentler as he spoke.

"You were victims of inner-city crime. Be glad it was no worse than it was."

We were not glad at all. When sixth period rolled around, we watched the receptionist's desk until she left to use the restroom. Hurriedly, we then approached her desk and flipped through the pages of the guest register. All guests in the building were required to sign their names, the date, and the purpose of their visit. Roxie was still certain that Sheriff Burley Haggard had been in to talk to Dr. Fitzbaum on the Monday after I had given Johnny's journal to him. That would have been October 11th. Burley had denied being there when I mentioned it to him.

It was amazing how many visitors did enter our school. As we perused the pages of the guest register, we observed a multitude of diverse signatures of parents, social workers, guest speakers, and salesmen. But there was no record of Sheriff Haggard's visit. The entire page of Monday, October 11, was missing.

On Friday evening I carried home a pizza, as usual. Dew was excited about watching the Hoosiers play Kentucky at eight o'clock. I had other plans for my evening.

Although I had never done anything even remotely akin to surveillance before, I had often considered how I would conduct myself during such an endeavor.

As Detective Brown, and launched like a missile into my project, I drove my borrowed car stealthily into the sleepy, little town of Pleasantville under the protective cover of darkness. Turning off my lights as I turned onto Franny Bumpus' street, I cruised quietly into a parking space several houses away from her home. From my vantage point I had a clear view of the Bumpus bungalow, yard, and garage. I was determined to know who Franny's covert lover was.

As I slid my seat back and settled into a comfortable

position, I began my wait. It was seven o'clock and quite dark. I slid a tape into my cassette player and popped a cinnamon ball into my mouth. My greatest fear was that I would fall asleep and miss something, so I planned on creating a sugar-high. A bag of candy sat beside me.

Strains of "The Phantom of the Opera" began flowing softly from my speaker. I reminisced about the summer evening that Dew and I had driven to Louisville with friends for the fabulous presentation of "The Phantom of the Opera." Although Dew's not exactly a Renaissance man, it was one of the rare cultural events that we both thoroughly enjoyed. I hummed along with the original London cast. I'm sure they would not have been pleased with my heartfelt contribution.

Seven forty-five. An uneasy thought crossed my mind: What if Franny wasn't even home? A light was on in the living room, but maybe she left it on to confuse burglars or people like me.

I decided to check her garage and see if her car was gone. Furtively, I slipped out of my car and quietly closed the door. Walking silently down the dark sidewalk, I lifted a silver penlight out of my jacket pocket. I was as ready this time as a girl scout on a camping trip; all I needed was a collapsible cup.

As I passed the house of Franny's next-door neighbor, I slipped behind the shrubbery that divided their yards and followed it to the one-car garage beside my target's home. Staying on the neighbors' side, I tiptoed up to the window of the garage and flashed the beam of my light into its interior. Franny's snappy, red sports car was safely parked inside. She was home. I was pleased with myself and smiled.

I then moved around behind the garage and glanced toward her house. The kitchen light came on. Franny was definitely at home. Although I had originally planned to do all my surveillance from my car, I suddenly felt a rush of lightness and courage. I murmured aloud, "Oh, why not?"

At that, I dropped to an almost-crouching position and crept to the kitchen window. Tiptoeing, I could see Franny as she took a container of yogurt from the refrigerator. Moving to the wastebasket she pulled the lid from the carton, licked the yogurt from the underside, and tossed it into the wastebasket.

I noticed that she was dressed up—as if for a date. She wore a snug, lime-green sweater with sequins across the shoulders. Her stirrup pants were creamy-white and as tight as a second skin. She wore spike heels that matched the green in her sweater perfectly. Her bleached hair was swept up into a French twist with tiny silk flowers woven into the folds. Large, diamond-like jewels swung freely from her ear lobes, and more bracelets than I own joggled on her wrists.

As usual, her make-up was heavy and her lips were bright red. Green eye shadow encased her eyes and dark eye liner outlined her lids. I wondered how much time she spent applying all that mess. Two minutes every morning always seemed to suffice for me.

Suddenly, Franny turned off the kitchen light and ambled into the living room. Moving away from the window, I cautiously crawled through some shrubbery and relocated behind the central air-conditioning unit closer to the front of the house. From there, I had a clear view of the front porch and approach to the house.

My squatting muscles seemed out of sync; I reminded myself to practice squatting more if I planned to continue surveillances. I couldn't believe I was actually lurking in the shadows, yet my heart raced with excitement. Dogs barked somewhere in the distance, the sky was jeweled, and the night air smelled of wood smoke.

While I was trying to decide whether to stay there or return to my car, I suddenly heard footsteps on the sidewalk. Keeping as still and small as possible, I craned my neck and watched as my heart beat in staccato. A man stepped briskly along towards Franny's house, but I could not see his face due to the darkness.

When he reached Franny's approach, he turned onto it and went up the steps to her porch. As he rapped softly on the door, I moved around the air conditioner for a closer view, all the time hoping she would turn on the porch light. She did not, but when she opened the door, enough light fell on him for a quick but clear view.

Aghast, I stared in disbelief and could not suppress an involuntary gasp as I recognized her visitor as my nemesis, Dr. Leo Fitzbaum! Smiling widely, Franny stepped aside as he slipped into her house. The door locked and almost immediately the living-room drapes were closed. At least they were discreet.

My head was ringing as I stealthily made my way back to the car. Never in my wildest dreams would I have suspected that Franny Bumpus and Dr. Leo Fitzbaum were lovers. Albeit they say that opposites attract, it had never entered my mind that they were engaged in a clandestine affair.

Admittedly, I was impressed, in retrospect, with their remarkable pretense of normality at school. I recalled how they treated each other with such courteous detachment. I wondered where the foxy Dr. Fitzbaum had parked; his car was not in view on either side of the street.

As I settled back into my car, things began to add up for me. Of course, he had come in time to watch the I.U. game with Franny. I recalled a Hoosiers' football schedule on Franny's coffee table when I had interviewed her, but hadn't connected it to Leo's great love for the Hoosiers.

Did he know something about Johnny's death? Was he protecting Franny? Were they in on something together? I wished Roxie were with me.

An hour passed. I tuned in the ball game on my car radio. My mouth burned from so many cinnamon balls; I should have brought water, but was afraid it would mandate leaving the scene and finding a restroom.

I wondered idly how Mrs. Fitzbaum responded to her husband's infidelity. Feeling certain that he wouldn't leave Franny's house until the game was over, I started my car. Cruising around the block, I saw Leo's white Oldsmobile parked on the backside of the square. He had discreetly walked around in the shadows. Smart.

Just off Pleasantville's main street, a lighted telephone booth stood in front of the public library. I wondered how the good doctor had covered for his little foray into Pleasantville. Quickly, I found Fitzbaum's number in the tattered directory. Dropping a quarter into the slot, I dialed his rural home. Mrs. Fitzbaum's sweet nasal voice answered: "Hello."

My mind was racing. "Hello, is this the Fitzbaum residence?"

"Yes, it is." She sounded like a social worker.

"Could I speak to Dr. Fitzbaum, please?" I spoke as professionally as possible.

"I'm sorry, Dr. Fitzbaum isn't here at the present. Could I take a message?"

"Well, I really need to speak to him. Could you tell me where he could be reached?"

"I'm sorry." She actually did sound sorry, "I'm not sure where his meeting is . . . but it's some kind of book-adoption committee meeting."

"On a Friday night?" I decided to plant a little seed of doubt. I have a mean streak in me.

"Well, I believe that's what the meeting was about . . . may I ask who's calling?"

"Professor Theatis Stone. It's the darndest thing! I was about to set up a meeting with my publishing company for next year's book adoption, but I didn't dream that teachers or administrators would meet on the weekends. We usually meet with educators on Tuesday or Thursday evenings—right after school. We know how those school people relish their weekends!" I was beginning to love lying on the spur of the moment. We signed off and I traced my route to be sure Leo's car was still in place, then returned to my parking spot down the street from Franny's house.

When the game finally ended, I sat up alert and ready to watch Leo depart but he did not. Naive me. Instead, the lights all went out. It was lovemaking time. I tried to focus on anything and everything except what was probably happening in the house. Certain they were immersed in the most fundamental joys of life, the idea of those two coupling was too humiliating to ponder.

I waited for an hour and considered what I had seen. I had witnessed Dr. Fitzbaum's golden metamorphosis. The man that I had watched walk up the sidewalk was no longer dowdy and jaded. His steps were springy and his appearance was jaunty. Instead of a baggy suit, he had been wearing chinos, a sweater, and some kind of running shoes. Love does strange things. When he finally departed quietly, staying in the shadows, and almost slinking to his car; he did have a sort of glow about him. I had figured out one thing for certain: I knew why Franny called him Dr. F.

Since Saturday night was "Trick or Treat" night in Pleasantville, I was glad that I had chosen Friday evening for my town snooping. My second surveillance would be far away from the little tricksters.

The problem with watching Peggy Benson's house was that I couldn't sit in my car. I drove past her home and parked off the road behind a clump of trees, a safe distance from the house and then walked back to her property. Shining my trusty penlight and moving from tree to tree, I worked my way through the woods until I was near enough to watch Peggy's home. Her porch light was on.

Sitting on a log, I pulled my windbreaker around me. The night air was cool with a hint of rain to come later in the evening. Twice I heard noises in the woods that made me uneasy. Shivers tip-toed up my spine as I gazed behind me into the darkness, but I told myself that it was probably just deer moving through the brush.

There was no danger of falling asleep in the woods. Crickets were in full chorus, in addition to a general cacophony of nocturnal animal hoopla. Fireflies dotted the fields like tiny pinpoints of fire. Autumn is the peak season for insects, heyday time.

As I sat in the wash of starlight, my mind wandered. I thought about Johnny playing in the woods around me. Had he caught lizards on this very log where I sat? I noticed how the coal company had mined right up to the fields around the Benson home. I wondered if Peggy was lonely, and if she had started working at the senior center yet. I thought about the value of the farm and wondered if his grandparents' good intentions had sealed Johnny's fate . . . how ironic. If he had not been named heir—would he still be alive? I dropped into a dismal mood.

Due to the flatness of the terrain, I spotted the approaching headlights long before they reached the driveway. Then, crouching low behind an oak tree, I watched. I wanted to know who Peggy's enigmatic lover was—the mystery man that Johnny hadn't liked.

I was taken back when the car that cruised into the driveway was the deputy sheriff's official vehicle. Why was Sonny Ray there? I figured he and Burley were watching over the Halloween antics going on all over the county. Maybe Peggy had been frightened and called for them.

I was wrong. Sonny Ray, out of uniform, climbed out of the car. He lumbered to the house with a six-pack of beer under each arm. So that was who came over and drank with Peggy! Recalling Johnny's dismay over his mother's drinking, I was consumed with anger.

Of course, it all fit. Peggy had called Sonny Ray that night; she probably had his number memorized. He came over and shot the snake—he's the only one who saw where the snake was. His story prevailed.

I suddenly remembered seeing him on the porch of the funeral home. He was a chain smoker—Johnny had said that he opened the windows whenever his mother's friend left. Sonny Ray the lover—taking advantage of Peggy. Sonny Ray—jerk extraordinaire!

Peggy met her suitor at the door with a smile and let him in. I furtively moved closer to the white clapboard house; I had to validate my suspicions. Whatever grand alliance they had, I wanted to know about it. It was no problem seeing into the house; the curtains did not close and the lights did not go off. Country people feel so safe from the likes of me.

Sonny Ray wasted no time. By the time I stealthily positioned myself for a peek, Sonny Ray and Peggy were already in a frenzy and entwined on the couch, kissing like two teenagers at a drive-in movie. As I watched him run his hands up under her blouse, I felt like a voyeur and turned away. I had seen enough to make me feel sick to my stomach.

The Benson girls certainly had a propensity for attracting lovers. Even at my age I was awed by the wonders of courting and mating rituals—those primal urges that keep the human race reproducing itself. But what unlikely couples they made; I could not excise the pictures from my mind.

Sonny Ray and Peggy were the total antithesis of Dr.

Fitzbaum and Franny. The intelligent Leo, that paragon of quiet dignity, and the rakish Franny with her quest for fashion statements contrasted boldly with the turkey-brained Sonny Ray and the frumpy, plain Peggy in her faded sweats. Dr. F. was so much older than Franny; what interests could they have had in common? Sonny Ray was on a perpetual ego trip; whereas, Peggy had such low self esteem.

What had attracted all of them to each other? Was it just the sheer horsepower of hormones boiling through their bodies that had united them? I felt totally depleted.

I made my way carefully back to my car; I had found what I had come searching. A myriad of questions flooded my mind: Was Sonny Ray capable of hurting Johnny? Did he really plan to marry Peggy and want Johnny out of the way? Although deplorable, it was the only way he could have gotten to the money. Had he taken Peggy out, and then come back and planted the snake, and then gone back to Peggy and brought her home too drunk to notice Johnny? Or had he brought the snake in—after he put an inebriated Peggy to bed? Did Burley know of their union or suspect foul play? Was he protecting his son? Had he investigated at all, or did he just take Sonny Ray's word for everything? The travesty of justice filled me with impotent fury.

When I reached my car, I tumbled inside and carefully locked the door behind me. As I turned on the ignition and lights, a square of black appeared on the windshield. Puzzled, I unlocked the door and retrieved the sheet of paper that had been slid under the windshield wiper like a political handbill. In large, bold letters the ominous words were scrawled: GO HOME, BITCH.

Chapter Ten

Undeniably, I should have been at least somewhat frightened, but I was absolutely not. Rather, my emotions ran to profound anger. Who was trying to scare me away . . . and why? Was I making somebody nervous? Was I getting too close to the truth?

The ominous note must have come from Boyd Slattery. His trailer was not too far from where I'd left my car. It would have been just like him to wander in the woods at night. Maybe he had seen my car's headlights approaching, as I had watched Sonny Ray's.

Most likely, he was the rustling noise I'd heard behind me in the woods as I watched Peggy's house. Someone had been watching the watcher; it was an unsettling thought, yet the irony fueled my imagination. Perhaps he had an interest in Peggy too—and happened onto me while watching her place. Or maybe . . . he was just watching me.

No cars had passed while I did my snooping on Peggy's property, so whoever left the note must have been on foot. I recalled the motor sitting on Slattery's kitchen table and wondered if he had cut my brake lines. He obviously had an affinity for mechanics. He could have followed us to Indianapolis, but it seemed unlikely. Maybe he had connections in Indianapolis and had simply made a call to some "Thugs for Hire" organization.

Well, his note didn't scare me. Instead, it seemed to exacerbate my interest in the Johnny Benson case; I was irritated and definitely not in my Saint Margo mood. I fought a powerful urge to rush his trailer, pound on the door, throw the threatening note in his grizzly face and scream, "You can't scare me—I'M A TEACHER!!" We educators have become immune to sarcasm through the years. Heaven only knows how many times I've been called a bitch; it's part of my job description.

Surely there was an explanation for Slattery's truculent nature and his profound distaste for visitors. Why did he not want me around? What was he afraid I'd discover? I intended to find out. I felt amazingly capricious and bold.

Sundays when the kids are home from college are pot-roast days with hot yeast rolls and rich desserts. However, when it's just Dew and I, we enjoy a simple brunch after church. As we forked our way through stacks of pancakes swimming in maple syrup and butter, I brought Dew up to date on the results of my surveillances. He found the tryst between Franny and Leo especially interesting.

"Well, I didn't think old Leo had it in him!" he said as he bit into a sausage link.

"Evidently he does, but I still can't see him with Franny. They seem so opposite. What do they talk about?"

Dew grinned, "Maybe they don't talk much."

"Do you suppose he keeps her? You know what I mean—gives her money . . . supports her lifestyle. She's single and can't make a lot of money as a school secretary, yet she seems to have everything she wants. She's always driven a new car and taken nice vacations. And she must spend a fortune on clothes."

Dew looked solemn. "It's really none of our business, Margo. Why don't you bow out now, and let the sheriff take it over?"

"There's still something I need to check out." Actually there were two more places I wanted to investigate, but I didn't want to worry him.

"I'm just concerned for your safety. After the car accident, I thought you'd cool it. And then the note, well, somebody out there could be very dangerous. I just don't want you to put yourself in any more compromising positions. I want you to stay out of the front lines."

"Don't worry about us. Roxie and I are in this together, and I don't intend to do any more investigating alone. We can take care of ourselves," I said confidently. It takes a lot to shake a teacher's sense of security.

"You're becoming obsessed with this, you know."

"Maybe I am, but it's so important to me. Never in my life have I wanted anything as much as I want to solve this case. It has become my Emmy, my Pulitzer prize, my Pillsbury Bake-off!" I knew I was being melodramatic, but I wanted him to get the point.

Dew laughed easily, "Just promise me that you won't do anything stupid. But if you do anyway, promise me that you'll tell me and let me come along with you."

I promised but didn't mean it. There were some things Roxie and I had to handle alone.

On Monday, I filled Roxie in on every detail of my momentous twin surveillances as we ate lunch in the privacy of my classroom. She was wide-eyed with interest, as I relayed the startling information and was most regretful that she had not been with me. She and Denzil had been out of town over the weekend celebrating her sister's silver wedding anniversary.

Roxie loved to dance, and I was certain that she had probably been the main entertainment for the evening. She had dressed in all silver for the occasion and had donned large silver bells in her ear lobes. Her dancing is best described as frenzied and combines rock and roll with disco and jitterbug. Sometimes she even throws in a couple of Russian squat-kicks for flavor. Crowds love her.

As I unwrapped my turkey sandwich, Roxie put together tiny meat and cheese sandwiches on crackers from a prepared lunch in a plastic pack. She supported my theory that Boyd Slattery had most likely left the note on my windshield.

We deduced that if Slattery didn't want company in the woods, then he must have a reason. He was hiding something, and we had a hunch what it was. We contemplated our next move as Roxie munched celery and carrot sticks, and I finished up with caramel-corn flavored rice cakes. It was a remarkably noisy luncheon but a highly productive one. As the bell rang, we tossed our scraps and empty diet-cola cans into the corner wastebasket; our plans were finalized.

At ten o'clock that evening, Roxie and I parked off the gravel road just past the Benson home and headed furtively into the dark forest. Armed with flashlights, we intended to investigate the area in a radius around Boyd Slattery's trailer. If he did grow dope, he wouldn't want it too far from his home.

November had arrived riding on an oppressive, scowling wind. Trees cracked and popped like arthritic joints on aged athletes. Most of the leaves had fallen, and their rustling as they were whipped around covered any noise created by our footsteps. The eerie wail of an owl caused us to stop and stare at each other momentarily before resuming our odyssey in pursuit of truth.

Cold air flooded into our lungs as we trudged along over decaying logs and twisted grapevines and followed deer trails through the forest. By some tacit agreement both Roxie and I wore dark hooded sweatshirts. We regretted that we had not darkened our faces to help us blend better into the night. Admittedly, we looked like disciples of Darth Vader.

Moving was tedious and difficult due to the darkness, but we slowly and deliberately made our way to the vicinity of the crusty trailer. Our biggest concern was the pitbull that Slattery kept confined in a pen in his yard. We were quite aware that a vicious pitbull could transform a casual stroll through the woods into a memorable experience.

Of course, we were much too circumspect to not have brought weapons of defense. As we drew near to the crucial area, I grasped the tear-gas vial that I kept on my key chain. It was to be my protection if the "Dog from Hell" were loose. One squirt was guaranteed to halt a dog attack and render the offender helpless. Roxie had filled her pockets with sizable geological specimens and planned to hurl them indiscriminately if necessary. We were secure in the thought that we could take care of ourselves. Jokingly, we commented that we had never been in military combat, but we had spent several years teaching in a junior high school.

We cautiously surveyed the area and relaxed when we saw the formidable dog pacing in his pen. His barks and yelps at seeing our lights were not as severe as at our first encounter. Possibly he was accustomed to seeing lights in the forest. Maybe coon hunters or poachers were frequent spectacles for his undoubtedly lonely life. Or, maybe drug dealers came regularly at night waving flashlights.

The trailer was dark; surely Slattery was not already in bed for the night. We moved in for a closer look. The area was as junky as it had been on our first visit. To the casual observer, it resembled a throwback to wagon-train days—definitely not the Indiana you see on postcards. The jeep was gone. It was an auspicious omen.

We wondered where our friend had gone on a Monday night. Most likely his hobbies ran to bizarre interests like wrestling alligators or bears. At least we knew he wasn't on foot in the forest and liable to be trailing along behind us. Surely, we thought, we'd hear his jeep if he returned.

Suddenly, a shot rang out through the chilly night air. Roxie and I froze in our tracks and immediately extinguished our flashlights. I felt the hair tingle on the back of my neck.

"What was that?" I whispered . . . although I knew.

"A rifle shot, I'm sure." Her voice was calm.

"Why would anyone be shooting a rifle at this time of night?" I asked and wondered if someone were trying to scare us. If so it was working; my knees were trembling.

"Maybe someone is hunting coons," she suggested. "My father and brothers used to hunt coons, and they always went at night."

"I don't think it's coon season; the fur isn't thick enough yet to be prime," I reasoned. "Also," I added, "they always use dogs, and we haven't heard any—except Boyd Junior over there."

"Maybe it's poachers . . . after deer."

"Maybe we should get out of here," I said nervously. "I sure don't want to get SHOT!"

"No, let's wait a while and see if there's any more shots," Roxie said soothingly. "If not, we'll be safe. Maybe it wasn't close at all. The forest is huge and if the wind is just right, noises seem closer than they really are."

That convinced me. We sat nervously side by side on a log and waited for about ten minutes. The shot hadn't been exceedingly close, but close enough to merit our attention. There was no more gunfire—only the moaning of the wind and the usual insect, bird, and animal hoopla. And they were carrying on in high style, apparently stimulated by the shift in atmospheric conditions. It was extremely percussive.

We finally resumed our search making concentric circles around Boyd Slattery's trailer site with each circle widening as we traveled. Our flashlights enabled us to see well for about twenty feet in each direction. Red eyes of horrified animals stared at us from just outside the fringes of our lights and then moved stealthily out of range.

When I had just about given up and decided to leave, Roxie declared excitedly, "Well, here it is!" She shined her yellow light over a perfectly cultivated patch of ground. Old marijuana plants drooped in the chilly night air, and a multitude of stubble showed where a sizable crop had been harvested. Our suspicions were affirmed.

Excitedly, I dropped to my knees and examined the illegal plants. It was the first time I had really ever seen a marijuana plant, excluding the plastic ones brought to school as part of the drug-awareness program. Although I was in college during the sixties, the age of Aquarius and chemical exultation, I had never had an acquaintance with marijuana.

Suddenly, it became disturbingly clear that we were in the middle of a very lucrative and secret project. People of Slattery's ilk have been known to kill to protect their valuable little farms. "We'd better get out of here," I whispered, astute enough to sense our dangerous position.

Ignoring me, Roxie said, "Look over there," as she motioned with her flashlight.

A small, ramshackle shed stood inconspicuously behind a thicket. From my vantage point, it looked like it could have been built by The Three Stooges. Jagged, graying boards overlapped on the corners and nothing was square. A rusty tin roof sagged, and a weathered and cracked door sat crookedly in its frame. Thick, twisted vines covered most of the front of the shack.

We approached cautiously, as if expecting an evil witch

to spring out at us. A heavy, rusted padlock swung on the door. The only window was filthy, but translucent enough to allow the beams of our flashlights to shine through. We pressed our noses against the dirty glass.

The interior was about the size of a large bathroom. A rough board table was built along one wall. Dozens of clay pots were stacked on the table and under it. The earthen floor was littered with leaves and trash. Except for the clay pots, there seemed to be nothing of value inside. Roxie and I looked at each other for answers.

"It's where he gets his stash ready to sell," Roxie explained knowingly. She smiled as if pleased with our conquest. We educators live right on the edge.

"We better get out of here," I offered weakly. It was near midnight and I was tired.

"What do you think we should do now?" Roxie asked.

"Let's call the sheriff as soon as we get home," I replied. There never was any question in my mind about reporting our find.

"Maybe we should call one of those anonymous hotline numbers to the state police," she said. "Then we could sort of stay out of it."

Maybe she was right, I thought. Burley's credibility was a bit suspect, but we knew we needed to report it. Creeps like Slattery often sell to school children. I'd talk to Dew about it and see what he had to say.

We walked towards our car, softly, yet triumphantly. Maybe we had uncovered the motive for Johnny's murder. If he spent much time in the forest, he surely had some idea what was happening at Slattery's camp.

Walking through the woods at night is a trial under the best of circumstances. However, we decided to extinguish our lights just in case anyone happened to be in the area. The moonlight was just bright enough to afford us to do that.

As we traversed diligently by moonlight, we were excited by our find and hopeful that it might shine some light on the case. We fervently hoped to be out of the area before Boyd Slattery returned. We proceeded silently along a well-worn trail.

Suddenly, I tripped over something and fell sprawling onto the path. As I got to my feet, my hand settled on a boot.

"What the heck!" I exclaimed. Roxie had her flashlight on before I could get my hand into my pocket. The circle of her light shone upon not only a boot, but two boots . . . with blue jean-clad legs connected to them. It only took a gasping second to realize that we had stumbled upon a body, lying face down in the leaves.

Cold horror gripped me as I had never known, and what emitted from me next could probably be best described as a primal scream. Although I heard it, it sounded as if it were coming from someone else . . . someone far, far away.

Roxie, always in control, shushed me by putting her hands over my mouth as she whispered, "Oh my God!" She then shone her light onto the man's back, and we both stared in disbelief at the blood-soaked circle between his shoulders. Not only could we not tell who it was, we could not even ascertain whether he was dead or alive.

I was so nervous I was literally hopping up and down, whimpering all the time. It's a wonder I didn't accidentally spray myself in the face with tear gas. Undeterred by my hysteria, the plucky Roxie slowly and deliberately rolled the body over while I grimaced. The next thing I knew, we were both staring into the glazed eyes of Deputy Sheriff Sonny Ray Haggard.

Chapter Eleven

The events immediately following our finding the body are still haunting and obscure in my memory due to my near-hysteria. Although I did finally settle down, Roxie said that she thought for a while she was going to have to shoot me with a tranquilizer dart.

Panic-stricken and stumbling, we made our way back to our car as quickly as two squat, middle-aged teachers could muster and then drove the short distance to Peggy Benson's house. When our repeated poundings on the door failed to rouse her, we tried the back door. It, too, was locked; so we found her bedroom window and slapped wildly on the glass while we called out her name.

Finally, a bleary-eyed Peggy stumbled to the door and let us in. She was in an alcohol-induced stupor and barely coherent. As she collapsed onto the couch, Roxie telephoned Burley Haggard. Since the sheriff was also the father of the victim, Roxie decided that he needed some back-up and put in a second call to the local state police post.

Actually, I did very little during the next few hours. For the first time in my life, I had lost the power of speech. A cold lump sat in my throat, and I could not swallow or speak.

Roxie, who thrives on crisis, orchestrated everything that transpired. She met Burley and the two state troopers who appeared and led them courageously to the prone body in the forest. She was there amid the flashing strobe lights when Burley identified his son, and the troopers marked the area off as a possible crime scene. She explained everything including our presence (collecting fireflies for science class), the shot we heard, and our incidental discovery of the marijuana patch.

In utter exasperation I stayed with Peggy and attempted to sober her and then to comfort her as she faced the reality of the night. Roxie and I signed statements declaring the events of the evening. A coroner was summoned, as well as an investigative team to scrutinize the area for evidence of homicide. I watched a grieving Burley slowly walk to his car to drive home and tell his wife of their son's untimely death.

When I finally got home, it was almost three A.M. I collapsed onto the couch only to be relentlessly haunted by the vacant eyes and gaping mouth of Sonny Ray Haggard. Eventually I drifted away and slept until the alarm unmercifully jangled at six.

Dew had a cold and had taken some medicine when he went to bed, causing him to sleep soundly. He had neither heard me come in nor missed my being in bed during the night.

Foggy from the medication, he asked why I'd slept in my clothes. Since he'd had such a terrible cold, he wasn't surprised at my being on the couch.

Unable to hold it in any longer, I told him the whole horrible story of our night in the forest and of finding Sonny Ray. It came forth in great gulps and heaving sobs that had been repressed until then. Although the police had not deemed it a homicide yet, I was certain that

Sonny Ray had been murdered. And, that it was connected to Johnny's death.

Dew was livid. His reaction was a combination of shock and horror. He wouldn't have been more upset if Roxie and I had been out robbing graves.

"I can't believe that you put yourself in such danger! What were you thinking about?" He rubbed his face as if to wake himself more fully.

"I told you we had two more places we wanted to investigate . . . well, Slattery's marijuana garden was one of them."

He paced the floor. "You and Roxie are not a Senate investigating committee! Why don't you just go to Iraq and overthrow Saddam Hussein?"

I smiled at the thought and made a mental note to tell Roxie. "We needed to establish motive!" I pleaded my case.

"You could have been killed!"

"Well, we weren't. We were extremely cautious."

"You promised me that you'd stay out of the front lines or at least take me with you."

"You wouldn't have gone and would have tried to talk me out of it. Besides, you felt so bad last night. You had no business out in the night air."

He sighed. "You know you have become obsessed with this case. I just worry about you; I asked you to stay out of dangerous situations."

"I know that my compliance has been less than spectacular, but I just want some answers. A part of me will not rest until I know what really happened to Johnny Benson and why."

He stared at me. "You don't have to turn it into the Spanish Inquisition. Now the state police are involved; tell them everything and let them take charge."

"We tried to turn it over to higher authorities, but nobody took us seriously. I went to Dr. Fitzbaum and the sheriff with my theories, and they both treated me like a scatterbrained woman having a mid-life crisis. Besides, since Burley lied about being in Dr. Fitzbaum's office, we don't know who we can trust anymore."

Dew coughed and looked wearily at me. "But it's not your responsibility. Let the professionals do it."

I knew he was right; it was the sensible thing to do. But a part of me knew that it might not get done right, if Roxie and I didn't do it. There was still one more place we needed to check out, and we would surely find some answers. If that didn't pan out, we'd probably step aside and leave it to the powers that be.

Needless to say, I felt as if I'd been run over by a steam roller, like Wiley Coyote in the Roadrunner cartoons. My whole body ached from falling and stumbling through the forest, not to mention the lack of sleep. But duty called, so I took a hot shower, gulped down several cups of black coffee, and headed for school. Postal employees have nothing on educators.

The next few days passed like a bad dream; I had trouble concentrating on my classes. Students filed in and out of my room, but I felt numb and went through the motions of teaching on auto-pilot. Gloom and despair shrouded my whole being; nothing made sense. I had expected the school and community to be in an uproar—a real brouhaha, over Sonny Ray's murder.

Instead, his untimely death had become cast as an unfortunate accident—a stray bullet from a deer hunter. There were no witnesses, no murder weapon, and no motive. The autopsy showed no evidence of substance or struggle, only a deer slug in his heart.

Old Sonny Ray never knew what hit him; the lights just went out. No one knew why he was in the forest at midnight. He lived alone and was off duty, so there was no recorded dispatch.

Some said he was probably just driving around and decided to check the forest for hunters illegally hunting deer by using spot lights. Others speculated that he was waiting to meet a married girlfriend for a midnight tryst under the trees. Although both theories were plausible, most people really didn't care what he did.

Roxie and I had our own ideas. We were certain that he had been set up. Someone had called him and sent him into the forest on a phony lead, then waited in ambush for him to walk by and shot him squarely and deliberately between the shoulder blades.

And maybe that same somebody knew we were there and sent him on our trail, wanting us to find him and take warning. Maybe they had given him a hot tip of a drug deal taking place in the forest. His car was parked not far from where we'd left ours; he wouldn't have recognized my old borrowed car. Maybe he saw our flashlights and was walking toward us when he was killed. Maybe someone shot at us and he got in the way. Maybe he was coming to kill us, and somebody saved our lives. Maybe we were becoming paranoid.

Boyd Slattery had an air-tight alibi: he was in the presence of many family members and friends at his sister's wedding in Evansville. Little mention was made of his marijuana crop. For starters, it was not on his property. The state forest was government-owned. Supposedly, anyone could have planted and harvested it.

Also, the amount was so small it would most likely only incur a small fine even if they caught him in the act of harvesting. The police showed very little interest in our find; they had much bigger fish to fry. No wonder it's so hard for common people to take a bite out of crime.

Although I was exhausted, I couldn't sleep. Nights brimmed with introspection. Even though I went through the motions, my brain was teeming and probably glowing in the dark. It seemed as though my body was floating somewhere between my mattress and the ceiling.

Nothing made any sense to me. If Slattery didn't kill Sonny Ray, then who did? Previous to Sonny Ray's death, I had just about decided that he had killed Johnny. He had motive: he would marry Peggy and they would enjoy Johnny's inheritance. Now what? I think I was probably clinically depressed.

Had my snooping caused Sonny Ray's death? The case had become manna to me, and I had been riding high on a wave of adventure. But I hadn't planned on leaving carnage and mayhem in the wake.

Everything that had happened could not have been accidental. There were too many coincidences: Johnny's death, Sonny Ray's death, the car accident, the missing page from the school's guest register, someone rifling through my desk and computer. And the sinister note . . . I suppose it wrote itself and blew through the forest, lodging under my windshield.

Roxie and I wanted desperately to solve the case. Our intentions were so noble; we were righting a horrendous wrong. Our plans were for Desert Storm, but it was turning into Pearl Harbor. The accumulated events bore on my mind like a stress test to determine the limits of my sanity.

I moped about tired and blue for three days. My usually hearty appetite had disappeared, and I had no energy for our routine evening walk. Of course, Dew was forced to be the voice of reason. "Let it go, Margo. It's not worth it. You've got to think about your health." But it didn't work; my emotions refused to cooperate.

On Thursday evening, Roxie and I headed for Stokely's Funeral Parlor in Pleasantville to pay our last respects to a man we had never respected in the first place. As we emerged from the car, Roxie said assuredly, "Keep your eyes and ears open tonight, Margo; we might pick up some important clues during our visit."

"Do you think Sonny Ray's killer will be here?" I asked quietly.

"It's very possible." Her expression was resolute. "We need to try to find out where Sonny Ray had been that evening."

As we walked up the steps of the Victorian structure, I noticed that I was finally beginning to feel like my old self again. Evidently the prospect of renewed sleuthing had dispelled my depression.

After speaking to Burley and Mrs. Haggard, we nodded to their two married daughters from Ohio. They had the same soft, baby-butt faces as their father, but with a prettiness and intensity that he lacked. Sonny Ray was the only one who resembled Mrs. Haggard, with the large forehead and thick glasses. She seemed very nice, and I wondered what troubles she had probably borne due to her only son.

I glanced about to see if Sonny Ray's ex-wife and two children from Arkansas had come, but they had not. I guess when she said she never wanted to lay eyes on him again, she meant it. Evidently, he had been as good as dead to them for years.

Custom mandates that immediate family stand in a reception line near the casket. In-laws and secondary relatives sit in the front rows of chairs. Close family friends and neighbors sit behind them. People like us were supposed to move on through to the back and mill around. Seated directly behind the secondary relatives were three weepy, red-eyed women—undoubtedly lovers of the deceased. Old Sonny Ray would never have walked off with honors in fair play.

Peggy Benson sat on the end of the third row weeping softly into her handkerchief. She was wearing the same gray polyester suit that she had worn to Johnny's service. Three chairs down from her sat Naomi Dymple, a beauty operator from Pleasantville. And exactly three seats down from her sat Precious Fae Parsons, a waitress of the Silver Dollar Saloon over in Oak Dale. I nudged Roxie.

"Look at Sonny Ray's women. What do you think?"

"I think he sure liked hippy women. But you know what they say: It's just more heat in the winter—more shade in the summer." Roxie continued to amaze me with her vast collection of trite expressions.

"Can you imagine how they found him attractive?"

"I don't have that much imagination; I don't think Walt Disney had that much imagination." We snickered disrespectfully and were immediately ashamed of ourselves.

"Seriously," I asked, "what do you suppose they saw in him?"

"Who knows, they might all have the same untightened screw. Maybe they were taken with his ego. You know he thought he was God's gift to women."

"More like a gag gift," I offered.

Roxie snickered again and I jabbed her with my elbow. Immediately assuming a thoughtful expression, she asked, "Do you suppose they knew about each other, or did each one think she was about to marry our hero?"

"Let's find out," I whispered anxiously. I was well.

Making our way unobtrusively towards the front, Roxie seated herself beside Peggy Benson, while I dropped into a metal folding chair beside Naomi Dymple. She was dressed in a low-cut, tight-fitting red dress and wore four-inch spike heels. Her bleached blond hair was piled high onto her head in a style that I thought had died with sideburns and bell-bottom pants. After sitting respectively for a few minutes, I began a conversation.

"Hi," I whispered. "You look so familiar; do you work in Maxine's Beauty Nook?"

"Yeah, I sure do . . . been there for thirteen years."

"It's a great beauty shop. I know lots of people who get their hair done there." She glanced at my hair, which I keep cropped short so I can shampoo, blow dry, and go. It gets trimmed once a month by a neighbor who has a home shop. Naomi probably thought it was butchy.

She nibbled at a hangnail. "I'm the main manicurist. Some days I just do manicures all day." Suddenly I became self-conscious of my short, unpolished nails and slid my hands under the purse in my lap. If we had discussed clothes, I would probably have crawled under my chair . . . in my denim jumpsuit and flats.

"I'm terribly sorry about Sonny Ray. Were you and he friends?" I gave her my most sympathetic face.

She puckered up. "We were more than just friends. We've been going together for almost five years." Tears started flowing. I patted her hand.

I nodded. "Five years is a long time."

"We would have probably got married next year." At that, she snubbed and blew her nose. "Terrible accident."

I agreed, "Terrible accident. Were you with him on Monday evening?"

"No, I went to the movies with Maxine on Monday night. He came over on Sunday afternoon and brought some movies. We watched movies all evening. I had no idea I'd never see him again." She wiped her eyes with a lace handkerchief.

I spoke from the heart, "We just never know what's around the next corner, do we?" She nodded and sniffed.

Quietly I got up, walked to the back of the room, and stood for a few minutes ostensibly reading flower cards. Then, as unnoticeably as possible, I returned to the row from the other end and dropped into a seat by Precious Fae Parsons from Oak Dale. Our annual teacher-retirement banquets were usually held at the Silver Dollar

Saloon, and she was the main waitress who served us; so I felt as if we were somewhat acquainted.

Precious, who had to be forty, still wore her dark hair in the long, straight look of youth—no bangs, and parted neatly down the middle. Decked out in a fringed shirt, denim mini-skirt, and boots, she looked as if she had come directly from teaching a class in country-line dance. A tall woman, she shifted her legs to make room for mine. Divorced for quite a few years, she was a woman who gave the appearance of being very capable of taking care of herself. From the size of her upper arms, she could have moonlighted as a blacksmith.

"Too bad about Sonny Ray," I offered. "What a nice guy he was." I side-glanced uneasily to the window to make sure no lightning was appearing. "I was just talking to him the other day. Had no idea that it would be the last time I'd ever see him alive."

She wiped her eyes. "I just can't believe he's gone."

I wagged my head in mutual disbelief. "There ought to be laws against hunting at night." She nodded in agreement. "Were you close friends?" I asked innocently.

This brought a fresh barrage of tears. "I loved him," she gulped quietly.

"Oh, I had no idea . . . I'm so sorry."

"He picked me up after work several nights a week. He loved my home-cooking." Her hazel eyes took on a faraway look and she smiled, as if remembering how much fun they had eating. "He always said, 'Nobody fries a chicken like you do, Precious Fae!'"

"What a tragedy. Were you with him on Monday night?"

"No, he took me home on Friday and that was the last time I seen him." She sniffled. "We were going to the drag races next weekend, though. He dearly loved the races." She looked directly at me. "Do you reckon they have drag races in Heaven? I'd like to think of him up there enjoying himself at a great, big, old drag race."

I assured her that Heaven probably had something for everybody. We sat quietly for a few minutes. Suddenly, she whipped out a plastic fold-out section of her wallet and began showing me pictures of her grown children and new grandchild. After telling her how beautiful they were, I soberly reminded her that time heals all wounds.

A few moments later, I moved over by Roxie who had been sitting by Peggy Benson while I had questioned Naomi and Precious. Peggy seemed so alone in the world; I wanted to say something to her that would help, but I couldn't. My honest feelings were that she was better off without Sonny Ray, but I couldn't articulate that to her.

We sat with Peggy until most of the secondary relatives had left. She told us that she had not seen Sonny Ray since Saturday night. He certainly had been a busy man; I guess he had to take a night off from his lovers once in a while. Unless there was a fourth lover who had not come to his service. And why wouldn't she have come? She'd surely have come . . . unless she had killed him. We sat quietly with Peggy until she left.

As we drove home, we were more confused about the case than ever. "Do you think we'll ever figure out what happened?" Roxie asked.

"I'm not giving it up until I do," I replied stubbornly. "It would be like a sky diver quitting when he's halfway down. What makes me so angry is that Sonny Ray was killed. I was just sure that he had done it . . . and he may have. I needed to talk to him. It's so unfair!"

"Of course, it's unfair," Roxie countered. "This is real life; it's not 'People's Court.'"

I agreed. There was certainly nothing fair in Johnny's short, tragic life.

We didn't go to the funeral on Friday. Dr. Fitzbaum

and Mr. Dupree went to represent the school. Frances Updike, assistant principal, was left in charge and flitted in and out of our rooms all day.

The faculty shivered in unison at the thought of Frances ever being advanced to head principal. It wasn't as though she ever did or said anything offensive to any of us; it was just the overwhelming amount of little annoying things that she did. It was sort of like being nibbled to death by a duck.

Roxie and I met during lunch and prep period that day and discussed our final move. She was not very receptive to my daring final ploy, but I adamantly argued my case.

"I'm telling you, Roxie, we have to search Dr. Fitzbaum's office. I know we'll find Johnny's journal in there and who knows what else. You know what a double life he's been leading. Maybe someway he and Franny are involved in this. You know how much money she stands to inherit due to Johnny's death."

"How do you propose we do that, Sherlock?" Roxie's tone bordered on sarcasm, but I pretended not to notice.

"I've got it all figured out." I was so excited I could hardly wait to tell her. "The school carnival is tomorrow night. We'll stay until everyone leaves and then we'll search his office."

"But it will be locked!" Roxie protested.

Calmly I said, "I've already thought of that. Do you remember a couple of years ago when an eighth-grade boy removed a ceiling tile in the boys' restroom, climbed up into the ceiling space, crawled over to the space above the girls' restroom, slid a tile over, and watched the girls?" She remembered, as did the whole county.

I continued, "We could climb up into the ceiling space over the guidance office, crawl over to the space above Leo's office, move a tile, and drop right into his office!" I smiled triumphantly. "What do you think?"

"I think you slept on rollers for too many years!" Her expression was one of pure shock. "Are you crazy? That's called breaking and entering!" She was wide-eyed with astonishment.

"Oh details, details. It's called creative investigation! Are you with me or am I in this alone?" She looked repelled, but fascinated. I stared squarely into her green eyes and continued softly, "I'm going to do it, Roxie. I've never been so motivated in my life."

"Napoleon wasn't as motivated." She took a deep breath and exhaled slowly. After a few seconds, a hint of a smile started in the corners of her mouth and spread slowly over her face. "I'm not wearing panty hose over my head," she quipped. Good old Roxie. I knew she wouldn't let me down.

She was thoughtful for a few seconds and then asked, "What about the night custodians?"

"I've already checked. They will all be gone by midnight. Then we'll strike."

Thus began the prodigious planning and mapping out of strategy for our final snoop.

Chapter Twelve

The annual school carnival is a grandiose affair and the main fund-raiser for the parent-teacher organization of James Whitcomb Riley Middle-High School. Riley Countians have marked their calendars and faithfully attended the fall extravaganza, which has taken place on the first Saturday evening in November for thirty-plus years. The social event of the year, it is strategically held during that span of free time between harvest and basketball season and has become the highlight of autumn.

Since overhead is minimal, the endeavor is amazingly lucrative. Proceeds from the evening are spent on uniforms for the band and sports teams, field trips for middle schoolers, prizes for the science fair, gifts for retiring teachers, and other worthy causes. Last year the P.T.O. purchased a big-screen television for the school, sent the academic team to Washington, D.C., and gave $500.00 scholarships to four needy, college-bound seniors.

Dew usually went with me, and it always proved to be an evening of food, fun, and fellowship. Friends and neighbors congregated and vigorously discussed every topic from pollution to town affairs. Education was unfailingly scrutinized and never found to be as effective as in yester-years. Much speculation was heard concerning the weather and crops. It was an evening out that few of the citizenry missed.

Fathers donned aprons, took over the school cafeteria, and cooked hearty food which sold for five bucks a plate. Choices ranged from country-fried chicken to bratwurst and sauerkraut. Bread machines cranked out crispy-crusted breads, while huge platters of German-fried potatoes with onions were carried from table to table as appetites called. Crocks of various salads and vegetables, sent by school mothers were available on a country buffet.

Teachers donated desserts: meringue-topped pies, fruit cobblers, gooey cakes, fudgey brownies, and an assortment of homemade cookies. These taste-tempting items were wrapped in individual portions and sold for fifty cents a hit. Diets were ruthlessly thrown to the wind every year on the first Saturday of November as countyfolk feasted on the lavish fare.

Dinner music was provided by the Blue Grass Boys, a group of local fiddlers and banjo players who performed professionally. Although they had never aspired to greatness, they were quite talented. Their repertoire consisted of blue grass, country, and gospel music. Requests were granted for old favorites, which they played with gusto. Without glancing at a sheet of music, they stamped their feet and performed as if they were entertaining at the White House. Some diners sat in the cafeteria all evening, never budging from their chairs, and clapped like it was the Second Coming.

After dining, adults as well as children enjoyed the many booths and shows that were stationed throughout the school. Dew invariably won prizes at the hoop shoot which was set up in the gym; old basketball players never really lose their touch. Discussions there usually ran to evaluating present and past basketball teams and remembering the all-time great players. They stopped just short

of having a moment of silence for the team of 1969—
which almost won the state tournament.

My favorite place has always been the bazaar and craft
shop in the art department. Dried-flower arrangements,
pottery, and wood-crafts purchased quite reasonably at
the school carnival decorated many Riley County
homes. Custom-made T-shirts and sweatshirts were spe-
cialities of the graphic arts students, while the industrial
arts department could never meet the demand for hand-
crafted wooden items. Enterprising people bought
these charming items as gifts for friends; hence, almost
everyone in the county was the proud owner of an oak
quilt rack, an Alpine wren house, or a set of tinkling
wind chimes.

Talent shows and lip-sync contests dominated the auditorium. Aspiring musicians, comedians, acrobats, and
dancers—both young and old, performed from seven until nine and never failed to sell all five hundred seats at the
rate of two dollars per person. As I strolled by, someone
was bringing the house down with a ventriloquist act.

For the older crowd, bingo was a highlight of the
evening, and the library echoed with the calls of B-12!
and I-26! Local merchants donated sizable prizes for the
winners; and cheers were heard as lamps, picnic baskets,
fishing gear, cookware, and dinner-for-two tickets were
won.

For the first time since I had been teaching at JWR,
Dew had not come to the carnival with me. Instead, he
was spending the night with his ninety-year-old father.
Since Dew's mother had died the year before, a house-
keeper came daily to cook and do chores. However, she
did not stay nights. Even at ninety, Ambrose was remarkably alert and healthy. He was able to take care of himself
and normally stayed alone at night. However, he was re-
covering from a bout with the flu and was a bit dizzy, so
his four children had been taking turns sleeping at his

house until he recovered.

The evening was cool, but probably typical for November. Our first killing-frost had irrevocably landed, creating a rather bleak landscape. The evening sky was slate-gray and the air was cold and damp. My navy and red nylon jogging suit and Nike walking shoes seemed just right for the occasion.

Since Roxie claimed an aversion to night-driving, I had picked her up. She had generously volunteered to spend her evening working for the cause.

So I wandered around singly at the gala affair amid the festive balloons and bright crepe-paper streamers. Not wanting to wait in line for a table in the cafeteria, I opted for a taco proffered by the Spanish club. For dessert, I found the toga-clad, Latin club's caramel-apple stand, and was soon savoring the delectable, creamy-smooth blend of warm, sticky caramel and crisp, tart apple. In all truth, it surely was the food of the gods.

Traditionally, my classroom has always been converted into a fish pond and frequented by the youngest set. Squealing preschoolers and primary-age children paid fifty cents apiece to cast a fishing pole over a cardboard seascape. The middle-school student government members, in charge of the project, attached small prizes to the lines, tugged in fish-like fashion, and watched the delighted youngsters glow over their catches. As I watched, I reflected upon the years when my own children had been enthralled with the fish pond. As the years had passed, it had required bigger and bigger fish to excite them.

"How's it going?" I asked Tandy, a sandy-haired, freckled seventh grader.

"Oh, Hi—Mrs. Brown. It's going great! We're so busy we can hardly keep up with the kids. We've taken in over fifty dollars already. Some kids just keep coming back."

I smiled at her enthusiasm. The seventh graders worked during the first half of the evening; eighth graders took over for the last half. "Keep up the good work!" I piped.

Down the hall, the home economics department was baking and selling cinnamon rolls. The heavenly scent wafted through the halls and lured me like pheromones. I purchased four freshly-baked, iced cinnamon rolls in a square, foil pan. A plastic bag around the pan offered a convenient carrying handle. My plans were that Dew and I would splurge on a high-fat breakfast Sunday morning and then do penance the rest of the day.

One of the highlights of the evening for the older kids was the haunted house. Every year, the science department went to extreme measures to outdo the efforts of the previous years. Closets were emptied of skeletons on stands and disgusting body parts which floated in glass jars. These repulsive items were on display near the entry to promote the proper mood for patrons. Of course, Roxie had been in the height of glory as she and Mr.Hartje, a fellow science teacher, organized the event.

Paying customers were taken on a tour of the dimly-lit science rooms, which had been effectively converted into a haunted house. Cobwebs, caskets, and various ghouls adorned the area. Strains of eerie music floated through the air as wide-eyed students were escorted from room to room and told hair-raising tales.

Roxie and her colleague made guest appearances throughout the evening. Raoul Hartje portrayed himself as a vampire, complete with black cape and fangs. Of course, Roxie was a zombie—his love slave, drained of blood with red lips and pointed teeth.

I wandered inside and found Roxie. "Good grief, you look worse than ever!" I said, slightly in awe of her creativity.

She was wearing an old-fashioned shiny, red prom dress and a huge blond wig. Gaudy jewels sparkled from her ears, throat, and wrists. Her face was chalk-white and her eyes were lined with heavy, black mascara. She had painted her lips bright red and made drops of red visible at the corners of her mouth and on her chin. Her fake teeth were perfect—six sharp points all overlapping her bottom lip. She looked like she had come straight from a blood feast.

"Isn't it great?" she said proudly. "It almost scares me!" She motioned for me to follow her behind a curtain.

"Are we still on green light for tonight?" she asked quietly.

"Green light," I replied eagerly. "What time will you be finished here?" Looking at her gave me the creeps.

"Tours stop and booths close at 9:30. We're supposed to be cleaned up and out of the building by ten."

I glanced at my watch; I had another hour to kill before we could start following our plan. "Meet me by the library when you finish." She nodded and I left.

As I wandered around, I talked with several teachers and parents. Although we are advised not to discuss student performances with parents at such events, it's hard to keep from it sometimes. When asked, "How's Junior doing?" We're supposed to say: "Since I don't have my gradebook with me right now, it would be difficult to be accurate. Why don't you call the office and Franny will set up an appointment for a conference?" Most parents lose interest at that point. It's sometimes easier to just reply, "Fine" or "He could work a little harder." Parents of students who are truly disconnected with the educational program usually don't ask. And those troubled students usually scuttle away quickly, dragging their beleaguered parents with them, when they spot a teacher approaching.

Since I had time to kill, I responded to a whim and decided to have my fortune told. The chemistry teacher, Mrs. Monarch, was cast as "The Great Swami" and set up in a private tent-like structure in the middle of the lab. Soft, Mid-Eastern music floated through the air to establish the proper atmosphere. For one meager dollar she read palms and made astounding predictions.

I dropped into a chair behind three other ladies to wait my turn. My cinnamon rolls were warm in my lap, and I considered eating one of them, but dismissed the thought almost as quickly as it was born. If Dew was going to get two with his morning coffee, I wanted two, also. After about twenty minutes, my turn came and I entered the tent and faced "The Great Swami."

As I sat down, I smiled and whispered, "Love your costume, Irma!" She gave no indication of hearing or recognizing me. Rather, she closed her eyes and appeared to go into a deep trance. A large glass ball sat in the middle of a card table that had been covered with a red velvet cloth with tassels. Her long, dark hair was encased in a violet turban with a large green jewel affixed to the front of it. She wore a gold brocade robe with satin cuffs and waved long, scarlet-red nails. I smiled inwardly: I was going to get my money's worth.

Finally she opened her eyes, but she seemed to look not at me . . . but right through me. She began making high-pitched nasal noises and rubbing her hands over the crystal ball. Undoubtedly she was trying to get a message from the great beyond. I waited patiently and was actually quite impressed with her performance.

In slow, drawn-out phrases she finally spoke: "I see a year . . . filled with great turmoil . . . I see family members drifting away . . . but they will return . . . and be much wiser." I smiled and thought how they'd BETTER be wiser, since it was costing us so much. She continued in her sing-song rhythm, "You will make new friends . . . during the next few months . . . and you will build . . . lasting relationships with them . . . They will bring great financial gains . . . into your life."

I could hardly keep a straight face. I bet she told everyone the same predictions. Oh well, I thought, it's all for a good cause.

Suddenly her expression changed from tranquil to troubled. She tilted her face upward and closed her eyes as if in deep, provoking thought. She began weaving slowly from side to side like a cobra while she hummed . . . all on one high note. Then, she suddenly and without warning dropped her face and stared hard into the crystal ball, while her long fingers waved over it. She then uttered in low, moaning tones, "I see . . . great . . . pain . . . in your future!"

Now I didn't like the sound of that at all! What did she mean—scaring her clients, I thought. Of all the nerve! I felt like leaving and almost did when she spoke again: "There will be GREAT pain and DANGER in your life in the immediate future . . . but all will turn out well . . . in the end." At that, she closed her eyes, dropped her head, folded her hands, and whispered with great effort as if all bodily strength had departed from her, "The Great Swami has spoken."

Taking that as my cue to leave, I quickly and silently gathered up my purse and cinnamon rolls and vacated the premises. Although I knew that it was all hogwash, it had given me an eerie feeling and I regretted the whole affair.

Surely nothing dangerous could happen to Roxie and me, as we searched the principal's office for Johnny's journal, I thought. We had planned so carefully: Stay in the building until everyone is gone. Hide in a cabinet until the cleaning ladies leave at midnight. Climb up into the ceiling and carefully move a tile. Drop into Dr. F.'s office and find the journal. Leave the office the same way that we entered, carefully replacing the ceiling tile. Let ourselves out of the building using Roxie's pass key. (She had been given one years ago to come in and work on science labs.) No one would ever know . . . how could that be dangerous? I shrugged it off and went to the library area to wait for Roxie, my accomplice.

Park-type benches had been placed along the walls outside the library, enabling bingo players to wait for games to end before entering. Older people seemed to harbor small bladders and made frequent trips to the restrooms. I dropped onto one of the benches, glad for a bit of respite. Admittedly, I was a bit anxious about our midnight plans. Although I realized that it was not a clever career move, it was something I had to do . . . the final step of my odyssey.

Crowds began to thin around 9:15, and by 9:30 all the games and booths were closed. Everyone left except the workers, who seemed to clean up rather quickly.

Roxie showed up just a few minutes before ten. Although the wig and display of fake jewels had been removed, she had not taken off her bat earrings. Her red dress had been replaced by jeans and a sweatshirt, but her face was still white. Thank goodness she had taken out the fanged teeth, or I don't think I could have spent two hours hiding with her.

"Come on," she said. "Let's go to my room."

"I thought we were going to hide in the guidance office," I replied curiously.

"I checked with Esther, the head cleaning lady," she said as we walked towards her classroom. "They clean the front offices last. We'd have to wait forever for them to come and go. They clean the science wing almost first. In my room we'll hide in the cabinets until they clean and leave. Then we'll have the rest of the time to move around and be more comfortable . . . just so we stay in that room until after midnight. We can even watch a late movie if we want to," she chuckled. I admired the way she was always so sure of herself.

"Are you certain that your cabinets are big enough for

both of us to hide in?" I asked in a nervous voice, still trying to shake off the ominous prediction of danger.

"Those cabinets are big enough to rent out!" she said jokingly. "Three or four people could sleep in one of them. They were built to store large equipment like microscopes and aquariums, but I have moved all that stuff to the closet in the back of the room." She took a deep breath. "We should be quite comfortable." We walked quickly up the carpeted ramps and through the double doors, which led into the science area.

It was amazing how soon the building was quiet, in contrast to the cacophony of the previous hour. The science rooms were hushed and dim. Not a trace of the dreary haunted house remained. We could hear the moan of vacuum hoses starting up in the computer lab next door.

Roxie led the way to the storage cabinets that were built along the walls on each side of the room. As she slid a door open, I saw that she was right . . . again. It was the perfect hiding place for us. Each cabinet was approximately six-feet long and three-feet wide. The top was counter-top high.

"See what I mean?" she asked excitedly. I applauded her resourcefulness. We climbed inside, Roxie with the white face and I with my purse and cinnamon rolls.

After settling in, we each sat with our legs crossed, facing each other. I quipped, "If three or four people slept in one of these, they would have to be on exceptionally good terms." She giggled and put her finger to her lips, signaling for me to be quiet. We waited. I made a mental note to remember to tell her what "The Great Swami" had told me.

After about ten minutes, we heard the cleaning lady drag the vacuum hose into the room. We peeked through a slight opening between the sliding doors and watched her at her job. She was rather plump, gray-haired, and probably sixty years old. A denim apron covered most of her print dress.

Before she began sweeping the room, she emptied the wastebaskets into her huge one on rollers. Next, she plodded around the room and squirted a green, disinfectant cleaning agent onto the countertops and wiped them dry with paper towels. Then, she bent down to insert the vacuum hose into the wall receptacle.

As she squatted, a loud, gassy noise exploded from her body. It was long and burbling; surely the force of the wind that escaped must have sent her dress tail straight out like a wind sock. It was exceptionally bad timing.

Roxie and I instantly shot looks at each other and simultaneously clapped our hands over our mouths to stifle our laughter; I thought I was going to die. My held-in shrieks and chortles volleyed around inside my abdomen and caused my ribs to ache from pressure. Tears welled in our eyes as we strained against all nature for silence. When I looked at white-faced Roxie, her hands were clasped over her mouth and her bat earrings were swinging in full force. She created an image at that moment which will be carved in my mind forever.

Luckily for us, the matron plugged the hose into the receptacle of the central vacuum system just seconds after she broke wind. The roar of the machine filled the room, and we were saved from being caught. By that time we were both lying on our backs, heads at opposite ends, knees drawn up, exhausted from the great strain of suppressed joy.

It was fortunate for the matron that she wasn't being evaluated that evening, because she swept the entire room in less than five minutes. Then she unplugged the hose, clumsily dragged it out, turned off the lights, and closed the door. Silence filled the dimly-lit room.

We waited inside the cabinet for another ten, long

minutes, until we were completely sure that the cleaning staff had left our area. After what seemed to be an eternity, we crawled out and stretched our legs. We could finally laugh, and we did until hot tears rolled down our cheeks.

Roxie said in her laugh-weakened voice, "I thought for sure that I was going to wet my pants!"

Security lights in every area prevented total darkness, and we were glad of that. After fiddling with the television set, we decided to forfeit the entertainment option. The reception was so poor that it looked like it was coming from the moon. We sat resignedly on the floor behind the last student desk-table combination.

"Did you tell Dew about our plans?" Roxie inquired.

"Are you kidding?" I retorted, "He already thinks I have an acute mental disorder." I had abandoned the notion of telling Dew and felt a bit guilty about it, but my reasoning was unfathomable to him. Success or failure, I had decided that evening was to be my final quest.

I continued, "He knew I was coming to the carnival and told me to have a good time." I grinned at her, "This definitely classifies as a good time."

"Won't he wonder why you're getting home so late?"

"He's spending the night at his dad's." I replied. "I told him I'd be home early."

"It's going to be after midnight!" Roxie countered.

"By the standards of the merry youth, that's still early," I said glibly. "What about Denzil—did you tell him?"

"Didn't have a chance. He left Wednesday with a vanload of woodcrafts and headed for Gatlinburg's Great Smokey Mountains Fall Festival."

"Sounds like fun;" I offered, "why didn't you take some personal-business days and go with him?"

Roxie rolled her eyes dramatically and said, "I have a

feeling that I should have!"

"You're not getting cold feet, are you?" I asked seriously.

"Naw, but we're getting a little old for such high-stress activity," Roxie volunteered. "I do hope you wrap this up in my lifetime." We laughed and waited.

At eleven-thirty we were both hungry and decided magnanimously to eat the cinnamon rolls. The fact that it was all we had eliminated all decision-making. The rolls were everything we had hoped they would be—yeasty, sweet, and loaded with cinnamon and pecans. We washed them down with tap water from the spigots on the science tables. On a sugar high, we giggled at everything.

"All we need now is a warm rock to stretch out on," Roxie declared. We felt as full and content as two toads in sunshine.

At 12:15 we made our move, carefully advancing down the dimly-lit hallways to the guidance office. The principals' offices were immediately adjacent to those of the guidance department. Although their files and desks were locked, the guidance office was not. In fact, it did not even have a door—just an open doorway. The theory was that it was always open to those who needed to come in and be guided.

As we stood in the middle of the guidance office, we looked at each other with apprehension. The security lights lent a dimly-lit, almost foggy appearance to the area. The silence was overwhelming. I wouldn't have felt so uneasy, if Roxie hadn't had that ghastly white face and fake blood dripping down her chin. I almost wished I HAD made her wear panty hose over her head.

"Are you ready?" she whispered to me.

"There's no going back now," I replied earnestly. "Let's do it." At that, I withdrew my trusty penlight from my purse and then parked my purse under a guidance counselor's desk.

Tall, portable cabinet units stood along the walls on each side of the office. In no time, I had stepped up onto a chair, then carefully onto a desk top, where I could maneuver myself onto the top of the cabinet. Sitting on the edge of the cabinet, I easily pushed a ceiling tile up and over. Dust particles filtered down into my face, causing me to blink and brush them away. Then, after climbing slowly to my knees, I stood up and shined my light into the space.

What I saw was a vast, sterile area that looked like a throwback to the catacombs of the Roman Empire. "Wow!" I said, "It's huge up here."

Metal trusses and beams went in every direction. The space was low on the sides and peaked to probably twenty feet in the middle. Heavy, riveted beams and thick, wooden planks provided walking bridges between the main supports. Sheet-metal vents and chutes broke the open spaces, as well as large heating and air conditioning units. A multitude of electrical conduits lay like silver snakes connecting all the heavy machinery, even climbing the beams to the ventilator fans that rumbled under the roof. I had no idea so much weight was suspended over our heads on a normal school day. It certainly gave new meaning to hiding under our desks during disaster drills.

Roxie called up to me, "Did I ever tell you that I have a problem with heights?"

"No, and this is NOT a good time to tell me!" I called down. "It's perfectly safe; we'll just be careful where we step." I hoped I sounded braver than I felt.

At that, and trusting Providence, I turned sideways and hoisted myself up into a sitting position at the edge of the opening. From that vantage point, I could easily see which wide boards would provide a trail for us. Crawling on all fours, I positioned myself in the direction of

Fitzbaum's office.

Roxie was soon grunting along behind me, as we proceeded towards our first breaking and entering offense. Actually, I was surprising myself; I had never been a risk-taker. My palms were sweaty and my heart pounded like a jackhammer. Silently, I wished that I had a nitro-glycerin tablet to slip under my tongue.

Suddenly, I heard a thump and a muffled cry. Roxie had slipped off our walk board and tumbled onto some insulation packed between ceiling joists. Enough of her weight was supported by the joists, so that she did not fall through, but it unnerved her. "Are you okay?" I inquired softly as I twisted to look back at her.

"I'm sorry, Margo, but I can't do this. It scares me to death, and I just know I'll end up falling through the ceiling . . . SURE AS SHIT!" As she resolutely spoke, she was working her way back to the opening. I guess she had shot her last bolt of bravery.

"It's okay," I offered charitably. "Wait for me down there; I can do it alone; it shouldn't take long." For some inexplicable reason, I was on a high like I had never known. I wondered if burglars committed crimes for the thrill more than for the loot and fervently hoped that such endeavors weren't addictive.

Roxie settled down only when she had her feet planted back securely on the top of the cabinet. With only her white face protruding into the ceiling area, she said, "Whatever happens, Margo, I want you to know that I think you're the bravest person I've ever known!" I smiled; it was quite an endorsement from "Roxie—the Invincible."

I traversed on, even though I knew I was flirting with disaster. But in some obscure way, I had a sense of being borne along by something great and wonderful. As I eased my weight onto the supporting frames, recent events flashed through my mind: the break in of my desk and computer, the sabotage of my car, the threatening note, and lastly, our drug find and Sonny Ray's murder.

Life doesn't offer teachers much diversion from the tedium of everyday school. In fact, adventures in a teacher's life are overwhelmingly vicarious. Consequently, when all that tedium is broken up by a few spurts of high drama, we record them diligently.

Estimating that I was most likely over Leo's office, I nervously slipped a ceiling tile to the side for a peek. Bingo! I was right over the middle of his office, but unfortunately not over any furniture where I could safely drop. I carefully replaced the tile, moved over three more tiles, and tried again.

This time I was directly over his desk. Thrusting my head through the opening, I surveyed the forbidden territory. I had forgotten what type of furniture was in Leo's office.

To my disappointment, there were no tall cabinets at all. All the regular filing cabinets were in Franny's outer office. Built-in cabinets with formica tops surrounded the room. File drawers were built into them.

Nothing was higher than his desk, so I decided I would have to attempt to drop onto it. I calculated that if I could hang from the opening, my feet would only be a few feet from the top of his desk. I knew I was in a precarious position, but I had come too far to go back. At that juncture, I moved onto the edge of the open area and tried to get my feet down.

I'm not sure what happened next, but something gave away and I started falling. In panic, I tried to grab onto a metal frame—part of the suspended ceiling, but it bent hopelessly and down I went into Leo's office. I tried to land on my feet and I don't know what happened. I did see my feet a couple of times—they were running scared .

. . and in front of my face when I landed with a mighty thump on my principal's desk.

The top of the desk was smooth and highly polished, and it served as a runway for me. Off I went into a sprawling heap onto the floor, dragging everything that had been on the desk with me. Two broken ceiling tiles fell and one bumped me on the head, adding insult to injury.

Dust and debris fell in my hair, as I sat awkwardly on the littered floor and looked up in horror to survey the damage. A bent metal frame dangled hopelessly from the gaping hole in the ceiling. Papers, pencils, photos, and I.U. memorabilia were scattered over the floor. All that seemed to be broken, aside from the ceiling tiles, was a shattered, ceramic coffee mug, that had been holding pencils. Admittedly, the office had the effects of a direct hit during a bombing.

Chapter Thirteen

Although I was shaken and horrified at the mess I'd made, I miraculously did not seem to be seriously hurt. Wincing, I slowly got to my feet amid the disaster I'd created, brushed myself off, and indulged in careful self-examination. Except for a banged knee and a scraped elbow, I appeared to be intact. However, I knew that my middle-aged body had recently become most unforgiving, and that I'd no doubt be unspeakably bruised and sore the next day.

Scanning the dim office, I nervously located the light switch and turned on the overhead fluorescent light. The room bloomed into life as if ready to assist me in my search for truth. Bracing myself, and attempting to control my trembling knees, I decided to check the open shelves first. Thumbing my way through stacks of magazines and pamphlets stored systematically in open cubicles, I worked my way quickly around the small office.

School handbooks and annuals were neatly organized in chronological order. Educational journals and literature from various colleges were stacked for easy access to interested parties. Obviously, nothing of importance to me was going to be out in the open.

The file drawers were not locked, so I hurriedly found the B file and sought Johnny Benson's permanent file. As expected, it had been removed. Things sure had a strange way of disappearing around Dr. Fitzbaum: first the journal, then the pages of the guest register, and lastly, Johnny's file.

Permanent files were started on each child when they entered the school system as a kindergartner. Each year, pertinent data was recorded such as: achievement test scores, intelligence test results, and final grade averages. Teachers, nurses, and consultants added their significant comments along the way. Records of discipline problems and attendance were computed yearly and interjected into the child's school history.

By the time a student graduated, his file was bulging with vital information; I've always wondered what happened to it after that. Possibly the old files became the kindling for the annual homecoming bonfire . . . how appropriate. Or maybe they were kept in a huge vault somewhere, just in case the C.I.A. or the F.B.I. ever wanted to scrutinize some hapless person's past.

Trying to think like Dr. Fitzbaum, I asked myself where I would keep a stolen journal and a possibly incriminating file. The answer was glaringly obvious: I would not keep them at home for fear of arousing the good wife's suspicions; I would definitely keep them at school . . . in a locked desk drawer. As I fully expected, all the desk drawers were securely locked.

Again, I attempted to think like my superior. I seated myself in his cushioned, swivel chair, spun around a couple of times, relaxed, and propped my feet on the desk. I then asked myself where I would hide the key. I certainly would not take it from the office, risking the chance of forgetting to bring it to school.

Suddenly, I knew exactly where I'd keep it. I would locate it in an unnoticeable place, where I could reach it from the swivel chair and lock and unlock my desk without standing. Plump, middle-aged people usually look for convenient shortcuts.

At the right end of the wide, oak desk, and running perpendicular to it, a formica countertop held a display of family photographs. The largest one, an old Christmas photo of Leo, his wife, and their two doughy-faced, bespectacled daughters, sat in the center of the collection. I carefully lifted it, and BINGO! There lay a small, brass key, and I knew exactly what to do with it. A surge of exhilaration washed over me at my success.

After slipping the key into the lock, which was located on the desk front, I was soon staring into Leo's private world. Expensive pens lay in the special section at the front of the wide, center drawer. Piles of printed school stationery and envelopes were stacked neatly on the left side of the open area. The opposite side held his candy stash. No wonder Leo was so paunchy! Had I not been so full of cinnamon rolls, I would have been tempted by the toffee and peanut clusters.

The top right drawer contained paper clips, staples, cellophane tape, rulers, and other office paraphernalia. The only item that seemed irrelevant was a plastic container holding dental floss. I couldn't suppress a chuckle at the thought of the dignified Dr. Fitzbaum energetically flossing away behind his closed door. Considering his candy stash, he'd better floss, I thought, if he intended to keep what few natural teeth he had left. Smiling at my own fleeting vision, I closed the drawer.

A deeper drawer directly under it held file folders full of perfunctory school agendas and daily bulletins. After a quick glance, I moved on to new hunting ground.

Moving to the left side of the desk, I opened the top drawer and found a calculator, two staplers and an electric pencil sharpener, but nothing of interest to me.

The second drawer held his appointment book, and I

thought momentarily that I had hit pay dirt. However, I was soon disappointed with its routine notations. Most of the contents were reminders of general faculty meetings, principals' meetings, and truancy hearings. Two dental appointments were listed along with reminders to pick up dry cleaning. Several meetings were described in initials only, and I wondered if they marked his clandestine meetings with Franny. Nothing was flagrantly incriminating, and I dared not take the book with me. Had there been a copy machine in the office, I would have considered making some copies, but there was not. Besides, Roxie was out there somewhere waiting for me. I borrowed a slip of paper and a pen from the mess on the floor and hastily copied down some telephone numbers from a list inside the cover of the appointment book. At that, I popped Leo's little black book conscientiously back into place.

Brimming with optimism, I carefully opened the last drawer while holding my breath. A telephone directory was on top, and when I moved it, my heart leaped. I had found what I had come hunting: Johnny's journal. I had been right; Leo had had it all the time and lied about it. But why? Who was he protecting?

As I flipped through its pages, I saw that it was intact. If it were incriminating, then why didn't he destroy it? If it were truly of no importance, then why didn't he return it to me? Was he blackmailing someone with it?

Placing it on the desktop, I returned to the contents of the drawer. A Manila file folder was the next item of interest, and I knew without consulting the tab whose it was.

As I perused Johnny's school history, a few interesting details caught my attention: His I.Q. was 120. Achievement test scores were consistently in the average range. Handwritten entries by former teachers resounded with repeated phrases: very immature, poor home life, often appears tired, grooming needs attention, has much more ability than achievements show, poor effort, a loner, lacks social skills, has potential, low self-esteem, talks loudly-suggested hearing check, etc.

Some newer notes were stapled to the folder in a neat stack. Their dates ranged over the past two school years. As I read through their contents, I was shocked at the recurring theme of neglect and possible child abuse.

Nothing pertaining to possible abuse had ever been mentioned to me, when Johnny joined my ranks that last week of August. Often teachers are asked to be watchful for suspicious injuries. And it is the kind of information that teachers usually share. None of my colleagues had ever mentioned that Johnny might have been a victim of domestic abuse . . . possibly neglect, but it's often hard to distinguish with older children.

However, unsigned notes reported bruises and welts, lacerations on the arms and face, a blackened eye, and possible burn marks. I was appalled and didn't believe any of it. Surely someone would have mentioned it, if it were true. And if it were true, then why had nothing been done to stop it?

Although I don't claim to be a handwriting expert, it readily appeared to me that all the notes could have been written by the same person . . . at most, by two people. One note mentioned how Johnny flinched when an unnamed substitute teacher reached for his paper, suggesting that he expected a blow. Other notes mentioned ill-fitting clothes, fearful looks, neglected immunizations, and frequent occurrences of falling asleep in class.

Another set of neatly-folded, type-written notes spoke of Peggy Benson's alcoholism and the resulting lack of effective parenting. Reports of telephone conversations with Peggy in regard to Johnny's care focused on her inane responses. Although the notes were unsigned, it appeared as if they might have been written by the school nurse. I put the folder aside and picked up a Manila envelope that had been beneath it.

Emptying the contents on the desktop, I discovered correspondence from the local welfare department and the mental health office; it was addressed to Dr. Fitzbaum. I read it all.

Also included was a yellowed newspaper clipping which gave a detailed account of Peggy Benson's arrest for driving under the influence of alcohol; it was two years old. Attached to it was a hand-written note listing several alcohol-related episodes: Peggy being tipsy at parent-teacher conferences on two occasions, Peggy failing to pick Johnny up after a school field trip—a teacher then driving Johnny home and later reporting Peggy as being too inebriated to drive. And lastly, an account of Johnny becoming sick at school. Although repeated telephone calls were unanswered, Johnny was certain that his mother was home, so the school nurse had driven him there. Even though Peggy was intoxicated, Johnny had assured the nurse that they would be fine—and that he would take care of his mother.

In addition, I found lengthy letters from an Indianapolis attorney and the Evansville State Mental Hospital. All correspondence dates were after Irene Benson's death in January . . . during that period of time when Johnny was sole heir of the Benson estate. Painstakingly, I read it all as I trembled with emotion.

And suddenly, the pieces started fitting together and it all became clear. So clear . . . I couldn't believe that I hadn't seen it until then. I knew—and a rush of adrenaline made me feel so light; it's a wonder I didn't float up to the ceiling like a helium balloon. It was a bittersweet discovery though, because I also knew that an inevitable, nasty confrontation was looming. High noon was just around the corner.

With trembling hands, I started gathering up my damning evidence. I could hardly wait to get back to Roxie to share my victorious find, when suddenly and most unexpectedly, a key rattled in the office's only door. "Roxie?" I said weakly. There was neither the time nor a place to hide.

My heart nearly did a flip, when the door opened and the doorway was filled with the imposing bulk of Dr. Leo Fitzbaum. He was wearing a green cardigan sweater over a madras shirt and brown corduroy pants. His face was grim and his gray eyes were filled with malice—but the most interesting feature about him was that he was holding a gun, a snub-nosed revolver, and it was pointed straight at me.

Chapter Fourteen

In stunned silence we stared at each other—he with his gun in the doorway, and I, seated in his chair with my arms full of his private papers . . . and Johnny Benson's journal. As most school principals, Leo had been given the gift of glare, and could beat me in a staring contest any day of the week. I'm sure my expression was a combination of terror and wide-eyed astonishment, while his was calm and feral. No surprise had bloomed in his eyes when he opened the door; he had fully expected to find me there. Rather, he displayed a calculated, sheer hatred. High noon had arrived.

I broke the silence. "You did it, didn't you?" I said and was surprised how calm I sounded, despite the fact that my heart was pounding like a jackhammer.

He changed neither his stance nor his expression as he replied calmly, "No, Margo, you did it. You finally did it. Just couldn't leave it alone, could you?"

"Was Franny in on it too? Did she help you plan her nephew's death?" My voice trembled with anger.

Rage caused Dr. Fitzbaum's face to redden, and he spluttered when he spoke . . . fat jowls shaking and drops of saliva spewing. "Leave Franny out of this; she knew nothing about any of it. She loved Johnny." He paused and collected himself.

Then speaking more softly he continued, "Sonny Ray

Haggard killed Johnny. He planted that rattlesnake in his lizard box . . . just as you suspected."

"He really planned to marry Peggy, didn't he?" I asked, "And live on Johnny's inheritance."

He nodded and spoke abruptly, "Sonny Ray was a womanizing bastard!"

"So you killed him to get him out of the way. I should have figured it out."

"He got just what he deserved! He had no right to move in on Franny and me," he said, still pointing the gun at me. "Franny and I have waited a long time for happiness. She deserved the money; Peggy's been nothing but a drain on the family all her life."

"Was she going to be the next victim, Dr. Fitzbaum?" I asked. "Were you going to arrange an accident for Peggy so you and Franny could have it all?"

He looked innocently shocked at my suggestion. "Of course not, she needs to be in an institution for the alcoholic, mentally disabled," he said confidently.

"Like the State Mental Hospital?" I asked waving the envelope at him. "Where she'd most likely spend the rest of her life, while you and Franny inherited a half-million dollars." I paused, then asked softly, "What about your wife, Leo?"

"My marriage has been over for a long time," he volunteered. "Franny and I have loved each other for years."

"She's just using you, Leo. Can't you see that?"

"You don't know anything about us," he replied angrily.

I continued on, "She's been using you . . . your influence, to help her get Johnny away from Peggy and have Peggy institutionalized. After she got her hands on the inheritance, she would have dumped you. Can't you see through her?"

"That's a lie!" he screamed. I knew he was volatile, so

I dropped the Bad-Franny theory.

"You were building a case against Peggy; you faked those abusive documentations," I said as I pointed to the Manila folder, "so that you and Franny could get custody of Johnny and put Peggy away." I paused. "Were you then planning to have Johnny sent away, too?"

"We would have raised Johnny and given him a good home, better than he's ever had. Peggy was a terrible parent; she was drunk most of the time."

"Maybe so," I argued, "but she loved Johnny and he loved her. According to the journal, she was good to him. Is that why you kept the journal, Leo, because it undercut your case against Peggy?"

He reddened, but did not answer. I continued, "Also, the journal informed you about Sonny Ray's entrance into their lives, didn't it, Leo? You checked and found out that he was the mystery man referred to in the journal. Then you knew that he had killed Johnny."

He glared at me. I continued, "Instead of turning the information over to the law, you took it into your own hands. It's called vigilante justice, Leo."

His face was angrier than I had ever seen it, and he mumbled through his teeth, "Shut up, you've said enough. Get up and come with me."

"I will after you answer two more questions, Leo." I felt that I deserved that much if he planned to shoot me. "How did you know I was here?"

"Easy, I'd been watching you for a good while, and when I came back past the school from Franny's and saw your car still in the parking lot, I knew you'd be snooping around." He glanced up at the hole in the ceiling. "But I'll have to hand it to you, I didn't think you'd go that far to get into my office."

"My last question: Did Burley know that Sonny Ray killed Johnny?"

"No," he said with certainty. "He knew that Sonny Ray was seeing Peggy and was worried that he might be suspected. He didn't want an investigation. We discussed it when I showed him the journal, and we decided to keep the journal away from you. You know how parents are the last ones to see faults in their children." So that was why he lied to me, I thought.

"Was Boyd Slattery involved?" I asked, hoping he would answer one more question.

"No, and your time is up." With that, he jerked the papers from me and motioned with the gun for me to stand up. I was about to be the victim of an act of violence. Although I didn't really think he would shoot me in his office, I was terribly frightened. His countenance was one of a deranged person and he was desperate. I decided to cooperate and try to talk him out of whatever he had in mind.

He opened the door and motioned for me to walk through in front of him. "After you," he said in a surly tone.

"Where are we going?" I was groping for ways to stall for time.

"To your car. You're going to have another little accident; only this time you won't be so lucky." He actually sneered at me, and I then realized that he had followed us to Indianapolis and cut my brake lines, but I didn't mention it. His eyes were glazed and filled with malice.

"You'll never get away with it, Leo," I protested. "Too many people know about you."

Suddenly, an ear-splitting sound filled the air. It was the screeching, but familiar sound of the school fire alarm. Roxie! I had been so wrapped up in my own trauma, that I had completely forgotten about her. She had seen Leo come into the office and had pulled the fire alarm. The cavalry was on the way, I thought hopefully.

Her ruse would have worked had she done it a few seconds later, but Leo was blocking my exit. As I moved toward the door, he pushed me down in the chair and simultaneously picked up his telephone. Keeping the gun on me, he quickly tapped in some numbers, and said into the phone, "Sorry—false alarm." Then after listening briefly, he added, "Yes, you know how we have been having problems with our system lately; we'll be getting it taken care of soon."

Truly it had been malfunctioning, but I knew who had triggered its latest action. My heart sank. It was over for me; my students were going to be seeing my picture on the six o'clock news.

An idea for my last chance for freedom then crossed my mind, and I acted upon it as quickly as I thought of it. As Leo replaced the phone into its cradle, I eased onto my feet, shifted my weight, and put everything I had into a swift kick into my boss's groin. He gave a mighty "Oooph!" and doubled over. As I sprang past the groaning Leo and out the door I remember thinking: The hell with my evaluation!

Actually, I was rather surprised that it worked so well. Women invariably received advice about kicking assailants in such a way, but I'd always had my doubts about its effectiveness. It's something you never get to practice. However, I was quite pleased with the results. One solid kick to Old Leo's safety deposit box had rendered him temporarily helpless.

As I sprinted out of the office, I hurriedly scanned the area for Roxie, but she was nowhere to be seen, and I was afraid to call her name. I wanted to scream, "GET OUT OF HERE—SAVE YOURSELF!" But I didn't dare. Leo didn't know that Roxie was in the building, and I wasn't home-free yet. The wide front doors stretched before me, but I knew they were chained shut. In fact, not a door in the building would open without a pass key. So I ran down the hall as well as I could with my aching knee.

Turning the corner, I headed down the carpeted ramp in full flight. By then, my knee was hurting in earnest, and as I grimaced in pain, I tried to think of a good hiding place. At the end of the dimly-lit hallway, I had to decide whether to duck into the cafeteria or into the auditorium. I knew I needed to get to a telephone, and I couldn't remember seeing one in the cafeteria. In my moment's deliberation, I glanced up the long hallway and saw Leo rounding the corner. He was stumbling along, but nonetheless advancing in my direction.

Opening a doorway as quietly as possible, I slipped through the stage door of the auditorium. Although there were security lights in the auditorium, it was completely dark on the stage because of the heavy, drawn curtains. The drama club had recently presented "The King and I" and had left most of their stage props scattered about. As I scuttled across the stage, navigating by faith rather than sight, I stumbled over a riser and soundly cracked my shin. It hurt like the dickens!

While I was sitting there in the dark centerstage, rubbing my throbbing shin, I heard the stage door open with an ominous creak. A crack of light shone onto the stage floor near me. My heart thumped wildly, and I felt the pulse in my ears. I knew that I should have sat still and melted into the furniture, but my survival instinct surfaced and I panicked.

Considering that I might get shot at any moment, I jumped to my feet and headed frantically towards the curtains. My plan was to jump off the stage and run through the auditorium and out into the hallway. In my haste, and due to the darkness, I ran directly into a large, brass gong suspended on a metal frame, a leftover from the play. Needless to say, as my head collided with the gong, it created an enormous clatter and announced my pres-

ence with a mighty G-O-I-N-N-G-G-G!!! The impact
knocked me backwards and left me dazed. I reeled and
staggered about trying to keep my footing. Momentarily
disoriented, I finally stumbled and fell sprawling onto the
floor as Dr. Fitzbaum turned on the lights.

When the overhead stage lights came on, the curtains
automatically opened. As I lay on my back, ears ringing,
head throbbing, shin aching, jammed knee hurting, and
scraped elbow burning, the lights and scenery whirled
around me. I wondered what a stroke felt like.

Although I could hear someone yelling at me, I could
not distinguish what he was saying. It felt as if my ears
were experiencing melt-down. Dr. Fitzbaum then came
over to my side and prodded me roughly with his foot.
"Get up," he snarled, "or I'll shoot you right there on
the floor!"

Stumbling to my feet, I felt blood trickle down my face
from my lacerated forehead, where a gong-inflicted goose
egg was emerging. "Please, Leo, let's talk about this," I
pleaded weakly. "Surely we can make some kind of a
deal."

I was hurt and frightened, but more than anything I
felt a great surge of disappointment wash over me. I had
failed to bring Johnny's killer to justice. Dr. Fitzbaum was
going to get away with murder . . . maybe two. I had
failed Dew, and Roxie. I was never going to see my kids
again.

At those thoughts, a great lump rose in my throat, and
I was suddenly consumed with guilt. I should have
known better than to try to catch Leo single-handedly.
My entire investigation had had about as much structure
as a nervous breakdown.

Dr. Fitzbaum was swearing and waving the gun at me,
but it seemed as if I were in the middle of a bad dream.
He kept pushing me roughly towards the stage door, but
my feet were like lead and didn't seem to be connected

to the rest of me.

Finally, I said in a defeated tone, "Do you want me to turn around, so you can shoot me in the back like you did Sonny Ray?"

Eyes narrowed with anger, he commented, "You don't know how much I would love to do that, Margo. However, it would be a little messy right here on the stage. Let's contain the mess to your car." His eyes gleamed evilly. Shoving me in the back so hard I nearly fell, he shouted, "NOW, LET'S MOVE IT!!"

Before I could take a step, a loud voice came from the PA system and a bright spotlight instantly shone onto Dr. Fitzbaum and me. And I would have recognized Roxie's voice anywhere as she boomed: "WELL, HELLO—DR. FITZBAUM!"

He blinked at the brilliant light and awkwardly stepped backwards. We both looked up at the control booth over the balcony, where the audio-visual technicians sat during plays. Roxie sat centered in the now-illuminated booth and was smiling at us.

From our vantage point, the control booth appeared to have been hijacked by an alien. Roxie, with her still-white face, accented by red blood drops, looked as if she had just dropped in from a distant galaxy. Seemingly enraptured with the numerous knobs and dials, she was producing shrill squeaks and whistles, as well as flashing lights. It was a perfect simulation of an alien spacecraft hovering over the balcony.

She continued: "THE JIG'S UP, LEO! PUT YOUR GUN DOWN AND GIVE YOURSELF UP. I'VE GOT IT ALL ON VIDEO TAPE!" Her voice actually sounded as if it were being transmitted from outer space. It was a truly awesome sight!

Video cameras sat poised in the control booth ready at all times to record school plays and programs. Blinking red lights on both cameras attested to her words. Leo's face flamed with rage.

With a jerking motion, he swung the gun up towards Roxie and screamed with impotent fury, "Like hell I will!" As he said that, he shot at the glass front of the booth shattering the plate glass and sending it flying in all directions.

As I hit the wooden stage floor, Roxie also ducked out of sight. Leo, in frantic desperation, sprang from the stage and ran up the carpeted aisle of the auditorium. Before he reached the swinging doors, Roxie's welcome voice once more reverberated through the air: "IT'S NO USE LEO—THE STATE POLICE ARE ON THE WAY!" I sincerely hoped she wasn't bluffing.

She wasn't. A few minutes later, as I limped up the aisle, Roxie met me and said excitedly, "The troopers have the school surrounded! I called them as soon as I saw Leo chasing you from his office."

In the following minutes, we watched together as a dejected and pathetic Leo, diminished to a mere replica of his former, dignified self, surrendered to the fog horns. He threw his gun down, submitted to handcuffs, and was led away by the state policemen amid flashing strobe lights. It was a victorious moment that seemed to call for applause from a watching audience; but only Roxie and I were there and we watched in silence.

As Leo was being driven away, we looked at each other with great relief. I smiled and said weakly, "I found the journal!"

Roxie, her cavalier attitude intact, nodded and said, "Yeah, I figured you did." Then she added, "You look like hell!"

I laughed and replied, "I feel even worse than that . . . 'The Great Swami' was right!"

"Oh, yes," she said, "I almost forgot. I also called Dew." We looked out to the school's parking lot and saw Dew arriving in his red truck . . . coming to rescue me.

Chapter Fifteen

Dew insisted on taking me to the hospital emergency room. After receiving three stitches in my forehead and being treated for various scrapes and bruises, I was released. Roxie accompanied us to the hospital, white face and all, and accrued more than a few side glances during our visit. I thought she might at least wipe the "blood drops" from her face, as a nod to convention, but she didn't . . . that's Roxie.

After delivering Roxie to her doorstep, it was nearly four A.M. when we finally got home, and as to be expected, we were entirely too wired to sleep. Instead, we scrambled a skillet full of eggs, made toast, put on a pot of coffee, and discussed the evening's events until dawn. As soon as the hour was decent, I called my kids and told them once more that I loved them.

We spent most of the day catching up on our sleep. As predicted, I hurt from my ankles to my head. My jammed knee was so incredibly sore that I could hardly walk, and it bothered me for months.

I decided that "The Great Swami" should get a nine-hundred number. However, a few days later when I asked Mrs. Monarch about her uncanny prophecy for me, she hooted with laughter and replied expressively, "I told everyone the same thing!"

At the arraignment, a remorseful Dr. Fitzbaum threw himself upon the mercy of the court and pleaded guilty on all charges in hopes for a lighter sentence. During the pre-sentence investigation, headed by the county probation officer, truth prevailed and all the grisly facts were exposed for public scrutiny. If it had gone to trial, Leo wouldn't have had a prayer, since the deer slug taken from Sonny Ray's back matched up perfectly with the murder weapon found in Leo's closet. (Roxie's video tapes didn't turn out too badly either.)

Leo is presently serving time at the Indiana State Penitentiary, where he is paying his debt to society by teaching illiterate inmates to read and earn GED certificates. Hopefully, society will benefit from Leo's poor judgment and lack of character.

After being admonished by the state police detectives, Roxie and I agreed to leave further criminal investigations to the professionals. However, they did not require us to swear on a Bible, and considering the gratifying results of our efforts, we aren't totally sure what we would do if a similar circumstance arose. Although we don't have any current plans to involve ourselves in other unsolved mysteries, we have entertained the thought.

The overwhelming exhilaration of uncovering pertinent data definitely left its mark on us. Although we knew that we were traveling on dangerous turf, we were motivated and thrilled beyond words during the journey. It was as though we were being borne along by some magnificent and fascinating force . . . something that called to us and refused to let us rest until it was resolved. Those fleeting weeks of high adventure shall always burn brightly in our memories as peak experiences. People who have been turkeys all their lives and then suddenly get a chance to soar like eagles, rarely are content to return to the turkey lifestyle.

We finally delivered Johnny's journal to his mother, and she was thrilled beyond words. As she cradled it in her arms, tears filling her eyes, the whole endeavor seemed more worthwhile than ever.

The upside of the whole thing was that it ended the long and bitter estrangement of Franny and Peggy Benson. Judge Boone Boultinghouse, a thoughtful, fair-minded man, awarded the inheritance to be divided equally between the two sisters. The farm was then sold to the Black Nugget Coal Company for six-hundred thousand dollars, a tidy sum by anyone's measure.

Franny sold her house, quit her job as head secretary at James Whitcomb Riley Middle-High School, and headed for the city lights of Indianapolis. After buying a classy condominium, she gained employment as a legal secretary for a prominent law firm in the downtown area, where I imagine she is quite efficient . . . in her work and in her play. I hope the astute attorneys never underestimate her powers of manipulation.

She was exonerated as having any part in Leo's criminal activities. In fact, by the time the sentencing hearing was over, she hated Leo as much as everyone else in the county. The attitude was profoundly pervasive.

In addition to inviting Peggy to spend a few weekends with her in the big city, Franny and Peggy took their maiden aunts on a lavish cruise to the Virgin Islands in January. Both Nora and Sadie Stanniger had shipboard romances with elderly gentlemen from Dallas, who were part of a group of retired podiatrists. Some say that by the end of the cruise, the only virgins left . . . truly were the islands. To the aunts, it was definitely a peak experience.

Townfolk claim that it served as a hearty tonic to the spinsters, who came home with rosy complexions. Reportedly, since their return to their hometown, their steps have been more brisk and their attitudes remarkably upbeat. The happy foursome plan to reunite for another cruise in August.

Claude Dupree, assistant principal, was temporarily promoted to main principal of JWR until the school corporation has time to advertise and interview applicants for the newly-vacated position. Since becoming commander, Mr. Dupree has spent an inordinate amount of time mapping the school and assigning new duty posts to all personnel. Disaster drills have become more regular, and all staff members have been assigned passwords in case of an emergency. Most of the faculty feel that the emergency has already occurred and pray for a speedy decision on the part of the school board in hiring a new principal.

Frances Updike, therefore, was forced to cover for Mr. Dupree as principal in charge of discipline. Apparently, her background as an abused child and battered wife has made her tough enough to meet the call. Throwing herself into her job with vengeance, she apprehends perpetrators with the speed of light. Her rather lofty ideals of perfect children made imperfect by their environments has been thrown to the wind, as she performs her awesome duty while terrorizing offending students with her cruel tic. We figure she could probably have disarmed General Patton.

Mrs. Fitzbaum, not wanting to become a pariah, divorced the unfaithful Leo and sold her brick ranch home. She moved to Columbus, Ohio, to be near her daughters, and believe it or not, has been working there as a social worker. At last count, she was dating a bearded Methodist minister, a worker in a downtown mission ministering to the homeless.

Peggy Benson moved into a comfortable apartment in Pleasantville and spends a lot of time with her maiden aunts. After becoming involved with the local chapter of AA, she has been able to work almost daily at the senior citizen center. Her share of the money from the farm was put into a trust fund at the local bank, where her bills are paid, and she has the assurance that she will always have sufficient income.

Burley Haggard decided that it was time to retire. He and his wife bought a motorhome and headed for the sunshine states. Loved and supported by Riley Countians to the end, they threw a festive "Burley Haggard Day" on his last day as sheriff. As grand marshal of the Pleasantville Christmas parade, he waved fondly to his beloved constituents as they cheered from the sidewalks and waved banners bearing the fond sentiments, "Good Luck, Burley" and "Happy Retirement, Haggards!" Word has it that the motorhome travels regularly to Arkansas bearing gifts to growing grandchildren.

Boyd Slattery still manages the Riley State Forest and is just as surly as ever. Although I'm sure he continues to grow his illegal little crop of happiness, the police are always on the lookout for more serious offenders. Since Leo admitted to everything except the threatening note on my windshield, I still award that bit of paranoia to the anti-social Boyd, protector of the infamous weed.

When Precious Fae Parsons and Naomi Dymple found out that Sonny Ray had killed Johnny and was planning to marry Peggy, they were incensed by the sheer ignominy of his deed and became quite outspoken in regard to his lack of character. There was no discord in their ranks; they hated in unison. In fact, they developed an intense friendship while discussing the common enemy and even included Peggy when they went to Florida for the Christmas holidays. While there, they formed an alliance support group and called themselves. "FLAPS," an acronym for: Finally—Learned—About—Pukey—Sonny.

Since Peggy is the wealthiest FLAP, she hauls the happy trio around in her shiny, new Camaro. In return for her chauffeuring them about, Naomi did a complete makeover on Peggy. Her new look, complete with make-up, curly-wedge hairstyle, and manicure is most becoming—not to mention how it has boosted her self-esteem. Simply having friends and being accepted is often a panacea for depression. Precious Fae taught the other two country-line dancing, and the three of them have a high-ole' time kicking up their heels on Saturday nights at the Silver Dollar Saloon.

Roxie and I continue to pursue the goals of higher education at JWR Middle School. Although we were revered somewhat as heroines briefly, those roles quickly dissipated as soon as all the brouhaha settled down.

I love the teaching profession and continue to regard it as one of the highest calling. In no other profession is one able to touch so many lives. Guiding youngsters to develop writing skills and appreciation of great literature is purely manna to my soul.

The single detestable part of the job is cafeteria duty, which can best be likened to a feeding frenzy in the piranha tank at the zoo. However, we do survive those unpleasant moments, and they make us better than we are. As my late teacher-father always said: "Don't be afraid of the tough times—they put lead in your pencil."

One fine, sunny April day during our spring break from school, Roxie and I visited Johnny's grave. It seemed imperative to wrap up the episode with a respectful call. Some deep, inner part of us wanted Johnny to know that we had completed our mission . . . that someone had heard his cries for help, even though it was too late. Someone had finally stood up for him. The truth concerning his tragic and untimely death had been revealed, and justice had been wrought.

In the soft and caressing spring sunlight, we were silent as we traversed the small, run-down cemetery. Skies were azure-blue and the spring breeze was cool, despite the brilliant sun. As we gently laid a bouquet of pastel spring flowers on the base of the headstone, a sleek, brown lizard that had been sunning itself on the grassy mound scuttled away. We smiled at each other and shared a pleasant, common thought: We hoped it was Ralph.

Epilogue

Why did Johnny die? Probably the reasons are manifold. Maybe he died because society has become too gentle, too mellow, or too apathetic.

Today's teachers are afraid to touch their students or become too involved with their lives for fear of reprisals and lawsuits. The days of teachers dispensing encouraging hugs and home visits are relics of a golden era long past.

We live in a time when law enforcement officials are no longer expected to be role models with sterling displays of integrity or even good citizenship.

Penalties for drug abuse are so minor that legions of adults continue to engage in criminal activities without fear of recourse.

Political corruption is so rampant that media reports of congressional scandals barely merit attention. Those same indicted leaders are often reelected by their constituents.

We shudder to see remorseful, sober drivers sent to prison for manslaughter convictions resulting from their drunk driving. Oh, we are angry for a moment, but by the time the interminable hearings and trials are over, we have magnanimously forgiven them. We are all too easy.

School boards and administrators look the other way instead of purging the educational systems of immoral and incompetent teachers. Fellow teachers often stand by and support offending colleagues because of their alliance in the local teachers' association.

Parents strive to find the noble character in wayward children and engage in the proverbial "seventy-times-seven" doctrine of forgiveness and support. They often stand by and ignore deep-seated emotional problems instead of consulting professional help, at the risk of dragging family skeletons out of closets for public scrutiny.

The court system allows juvenile offenders to remain in the main stream of education and to harass fellow students and teachers. Thus, schools have become half-way houses teeming with juvenile delinquents and emotionally disturbed students, like time-bombs just waiting to explode. Laws protecting their rights enable them to disrupt class and continually interrupt the educational process. The distractions caused by this protected minority take up so much of the teachers' time, that the well-behaved students who truly desire to learn lose their rights to a good education. It is a frustrating time for dedicated teachers, this time of minority rule . . . this time when schools are no longer safe places for children.

It is a time when laws allow alcoholic and drug-abusing parents to walk out of hospitals carrying their progeny and possible future victims.

We live in a society that fosters welfare dependency, often borne with side effects of low self-esteem and depression. Social services, busy with mountains of paperwork, too often leave children struggling to swim in homes where subterranean tides threaten daily to pull them under.

We are a forgiving society, a sect of believers in the "one more chance" doctrine. We can't bear to see children taken from the arms of weeping mothers—no matter what offenses those mothers have committed.

Our society has fallen to the lowest level of morality; it is a time of unparalleled crime. Broken homes and dysfunctional families are rapidly becoming the norm. Child abuse and wife battering are so commonplace that we have become desensitized to their depravity. Those kids who survive violent homes often become emotionally and psychologically damaged beyond repair. Legions of children, physically and emotionally abandoned by their parents, are parenting themselves. Neighbors and churches often choose to turn their heads when children live in flawed homes.

One million cases of abuse and neglect were confirmed in our country last year, according to current statistics. Almost half of the 1,300 children who died of abuse lived in homes where child abuse had previously been reported to authorities. The national policy has been reunification of the family—at almost any cost. It is a system where a parent's rights are placed above a child's rights. The fate of today's children lies with all of us.

Our sin is omission; our crime is complacency.

Maybe we all killed Johnny.